The Little
MATCHMAKERS

SANDRA LEA BURKITT

Copyright © 2022 Sandra Lea Burkitt

All rights reserved. No part of this book may be reproduced, stored, or transmitted by any means—whether auditory, graphic, mechanical, or electronic—without written permission of both publisher and author, except in the case of brief excerpts used in critical articles and reviews. Unauthorized reproduction of any part of this work is illegal and is punishable by law.

ISBN: 979-8-88640-058-8 (sc)
ISBN: 979-8-88640-059-5 (hc)
ISBN: 979-8-88640-060-1 (e)

Because of the dynamic nature of the Internet, any web addresses or links contained in this book may have changed since publication and may no longer be valid. The views expressed in this work are solely those of the author and do not necessarily reflect the views of the publisher, and the publisher hereby disclaims any responsibility for them.

One Galleria Blvd., Suite 1900, Metairie, LA 70001
1-888-421-2397

By the same author:

A Stroke of Courage
Flowers for Mrs. Claus

With deepest love and affection to my amazing daughters,
Krystol and Chantel,
who gave me the characters of Jennifer and Pip.

Contents

Chapter 1	When Jennifer Became Worried	1
Chapter 2	When Jennifer Found the Solution	12
Chapter 3	When Jennifer Stayed In Her Room	24
Chapter 4	When Jennifer Met Harry	34
Chapter 5	When Jennifer Took Pip to the Dentist	44
Chapter 6	When Jennifer Slept	51
Chapter 7	When Jennifer's Plans Went Amiss	60
Chapter 8	When Jennifer Schemed Again	72
Chapter 9	When Jennifer Wasn't Allowed To Go	82
Chapter 10	When Jennifer Needed Money	93
Chapter 11	When Jennifer Got Caught	104
Chapter 12	When Jennifer's Lost Cause Was Found	113
Chapter 13	When Jennifer Wished Her Lost Cause Was Still Lost	121
Chapter 14	When Jennifer Would Have Been Proud of Me	132
Chapter 15	When Jennifer Wanted Harry	145
Chapter 16	When Jennifer Woke Up	158

Chapter One

WHEN JENNIFER BECAME WORRIED

Jennifer is my big sister, and of course she has to get in her two cents worth. She says my story should start when our dad walked out on us, but I was just a baby then and I don't remember. I can hardly write about something I don't remember, can I?

Jennifer always said boys need dads to teach them things and it was because I didn't have a dad to shape me up that I was so scared of everything—even my own shadow. (But I wasn't really afraid of my shadow—it was only that one time I jumped and Jennifer saw me.)

But, as Jen said, I at least had her to teach me all the important stuff—like girls know everything and boys, like me, know nothing and that's why girls are the bosses and boys have to do everything girls tell them to do. Well, I was little then, and I actually believed her. That is, until Harry came into my life.

Anyway, for me my story began with Jennifer's friend, Brenda, getting ready to move away and Brenda's Mom having a garage sale that wasn't a garage sale. Jennifer was almost 12 and in grade 6 so we still went to the same school and therefore was still in charge of my every move while Mom was at work. My story takes place before there were cell phones, before there was internet, before there were

I-pods, even before there was satellite television, and before there was a computer in every home.

It was snowing like crazy the day of the garage sale, and I was all alone in the schoolyard. I had a bright red snowsuit on which must have showed up like a beacon in the midst of all that swirling snow. The wind was howling around the corners of the school and I was *freezing*. With hands clumsy in their blue woolen mittens, I tugged at my hood, hoping to pull it down over my cold forehead. It didn't work.

There was no one around. The school buses had left long ago. The kids who walked home had left, hurriedly, long before that. I longed to be home where it was warm and safe, but I couldn't go without Jennifer. She had the house key.

I turned and walked slowly back towards the school, bracing myself miserably against the cold January wind. I was just a little bit nervous. Nervous, remember, not afraid. There *is* a difference! I simply didn't like being alone like this. I was not used to being alone like this. I whirled around, suddenly, half expecting to find someone there. No one was. No monster. No boogie-man. Not even Jennifer. Where *was* she?

I went up the steps to the door and tried, for the dozenth time, to open it. The wind was still too strong and I still wasn't strong enough. I felt *very* small. A heaviness seemed to fall on me as I plodded back into the empty schoolyard. There was something spooky about an empty schoolyard in the middle of a snowstorm. The back of my neck tingled.

Where was Jennifer? Had she gone home without me? Had she forgotten her own little brother? Had something terrible happened to her? Should I go home alone and phone Mom? But Jennifer had the key! I'd have to wait.

My hands and feet were beginning to hurt with the cold when I saw a man walking down the street towards me. The man was looking at me. I stood perfectly still. Maybe this man had grabbed Jennifer and was coming for me. I'd heard of things like that.

The man slowed his pace. He smiled. I could hardly breathe. I could actually hear my own pulse beating in my ears. Should I run? Should I hide? But for some strange reason I couldn't move!

But the man just waved and walked on.

I breathed again.

I walked behind the school, out of the wind, and felt less cold. Here, at least, the wind could not swirl the snow all around me and snatch my breath away. I pulled my scarf up over my nose and mouth. It would get all snotty and yucky now, but I didn't care. It was better than freezing. Then I heard voices and I peeked around the corner.

Jennifer and her friend, Brenda, were walking towards the street. *They weren't even looking for me!*

I tore across the schoolyard and out in front of the girls.

"Oh, there you are, Pip," said Jennifer. "I was wondering."

"You were not!" I screamed and aimed a stiff kick at Jennifer's shin.

Jennifer howled and began hopping around on one foot as I raced out of the school yard and down the snow covered sidewalk.

"Pip!" yelled Jennifer. "You come back here!"

But I was running for all I was worth. Suddenly, my feet landed on a patch of ice and went skidding out from under me. I lay still, while the wind threw snow in my face, and waited for Jennifer.

"Pip!" yelled Jennifer as she and Brenda ran towards me. "Pip! Are you all right?"

Jennifer knelt beside me and I nodded numbly.

"What did you kick me for?" she demanded angrily. "You know you should never kick anyone."

"You left me alone!" I sobbed and wiped the tears away with my snowy mitten. "I was cold and I...I thought you'd gone."

"Pip, you know I wouldn't go home without you," said Jennifer.

"Wouldn't you?" I cried. "You were just going to walk off without even looking for me!"

"I was not!"

"Were, too!" I sniffed.

"Sorry, Pip," said Jennifer, but I didn't think she sounded sorry at all. "I was all upset about Brenda and I guess I kinda forgot. You know…"

I didn't know.

"Come on, Pip," said Jennifer, helping me up and giving me a tissue. "We gotta go."

I dried my eyes, blew my nose, and pulled my soggy scarf back up over my nose.

"Why were you so late, anyway?" I asked.

"Because we had a lot of talking to do," Jennifer said. "Brenda's moving away tomorrow, remember? We'll probably never…ever… see each other…you know."

I didn't know.

"Where you movin' to?" I asked.

"A farm out west," Brenda said as they began walking again. "It's a great big one. We're going to live with my grandparents and help with the farming."

"You mean cows and horses and stuff?" I asked as I trudged along behind.

"Nah. No animals," replied Brenda. "My Grandpa raises wheat and barley. Hundreds of acres of it."

"You mean you'll get to ride in one of those big machines it shows on that cereal commercial?" I asked excitedly.

"I don't know. I guess so," said Brenda who seemed, amazingly, to be totally uninterested.

"Wow! Cool!" I exclaimed, wondering if Brenda liked me well enough to invite me out for a visit. Probably not.

We were at the corner now and I waited for the girls to say good-bye. I wanted to rush home and get warm but first I wanted to go into the little store across the street and spend my last twenty-five cents. I stared at the store longingly and waited. And waited. But the girls didn't say good-bye. They just stared, first at each other, then at their boots.

"Let's walk Brenda home," suggested Jennifer at last.

"My feet are frozen!" I groaned.

"Pip! Please!" begged Jennifer. "It's for the *very last time*!"

"But I'm freezing to death, Jennifer! I'll get pneumonia!" I wailed.

Jennifer put her hands on my shoulders and met my blue eyes with her big brown ones. "Please, Pip!"

I sighed. I could not resist Jennifer. I never could.

"Thanks, Pip," said Jennifer, dropping her hands and turning quickly back to Brenda. "And you can't get pneumonia from being cold because it's a germ. It's hypothermia you get from being cold."

"Then I'll get that," I asserted.

"Probably, but it's for a good cause," she said as they turned the corner and began the two block walk to Brenda's.

I trudged miserably along behind the girls. As we crossed the next street I could see there was an unusual amount of activity. Cars were lined up on both sides of the street. People were jumping in and out of vehicles and coming and going all over every which way. Most people were carrying something. A box. A bag. A lamp. A chair. A lawn mower. A barbecue--in *January*?

"What's going on?" I asked, but the girls were not listening.

The closer we got to Brenda's house, the more crowded the snowy sidewalk became. People were everywhere, and most walked with their heads held down against the wind and their arms wrapped snugly around their treasure. They couldn't see where they were going much less little me who was trudging along behind the older and taller girls.

As I leapt out of yet another person's way, I yelled, "Hey, lemme go in front, will ya?"

I squiggled between the girls just as a sofa loomed in front of me. "Hit the decks!" I cried, throwing myself into a snowdrift to avoid being slammed in the head. "Watch where you're going, will ya!" I yelled after the men, but no one even noticed me. I picked myself up and ran after the girls who had again forgotten me and were tramping up the front walk to Brenda's house. Dodging people and snow drifts I caught up to them just as they opened the door.

"What's going on, anyway?" I asked.

"I told you," sighed Jennifer. "They're moving," and she pointed to the sign on the house: 'GARAGE SALE'.

With great difficulty we edged our way through the entrance hall.

People were going in and coming out of the living room, and going up and coming down the staircase. It reminded me of a department store at Christmas time.

"But this isn't the garage, Jennifer," I said, tugging at her parka.

"What?"

"Garage Sale. This isn't the garage!"

"Oh, Pip!" groaned Jennifer.

Well, it wasn't, I thought, as we finally squeezed into the living room.

We found Brenda's mother there, amid a pile of boxes and crates. She had a notepad and a large chocolate box beside her. She was arguing with an elderly lady who held the ugliest statue I had ever seen. It seemed to be part animal and part human. It had huge horns and a big mouth with ugly sharp teeth sticking out. It's ears were long and pointy and it had long skinny sharp fingers that hung down to it's knees.

"No, my dear," I heard Brenda's mother say. "It's not five dollars, it's fifty. See? It's written right on that sticker."

"Well, I don't have fifty," the elderly lady snapped. "You want to sell it or don't you? I have a taxi waiting so make up your mind."

"What's she want it for anyway?" I asked. "It's *ugly*!"

"Pip!" cried Jennifer, turning a little pink and staring up at the ceiling.

"Well, it is," I insisted, because it was.

"Be quiet!" scolded Jennifer. She gave me a dig in the ribs with her elbow.

I left and walked over to some boxes that were piled in the corner. "What's in these?" I asked.

Jennifer yanked me back. "None of your business," she growled.

"It's okay, Jennifer," Brenda said. "That's what we're taking with us."

"That's *all* you're taking? Where are your beds?" I cried, imagining them sleeping in a cold bare corner of a strange room.

"We don't need any furniture at Grandma's. We're just taking our clothes and stuff. You know."

I didn't know. I was beginning to wonder if I wanted to know. Not taking your bed! The idea was horrifying. "Gee," was all I could think of to say. I turned back to the old lady and Brenda's mother who was now putting a ten-dollar bill into her chocolate box. The elderly lady smiled happily and hurried off, cradling the statue in her arms.

"What is that thing anyway," I asked, "some kinda animal or what?"

Brenda shrugged and went over to her mother. Jennifer and I followed.

"Oh, Brenda," her mother said, "you're home. I was beginning to worry."

"We were just talking, Mom," Brenda assured her.

"Yes. Yes, of course," her mother said, and I could see that she had tears in her eyes. "Hello, Jennifer. Hello, Philip. So nice of you to walk Brenda home. Did you see my Herman go?"

Brenda nodded and now I saw that her mother's chin was trembling.

"My dear, dear Herman!" she cried. "I hope that lady gives him a good home. I'll be lost without him. Whatever shall I do? All my lovely things gone." She sighed and then straightened her shoulders. "And all I got for him was a measly ten dollars!"

"Sorry, Mom."

"Ah well, never mind," she said, wiping her eyes. "You children look half frozen. And it's so cold in here! I just don't understand people. This weather and they keep opening doors! Now go get some hot chocolate. That'll warm you up."

"Sure, Mom."

"But how can they get in to buy stuff if they don't open the—"

"*PIP!*" growled Jennifer between clenched teeth.

"Well, how can they? Or get back out, too."

Jennifer elbowed me again and then, smiling weakly at Brenda's mother, hurried into the kitchen behind Brenda. I followed. Hot chocolate sounded good. But when we entered the kitchen, the kitchen was gone. Only the cupboards and the sink remained and, for me, that did not make a kitchen.

"Gee, Brenda," said Jennifer, "it doesn't seem like your house anymore."

Brenda nodded glumly.

I began opening cupboard doors. They were all empty. "I bet you don't even *have* any hot chocolate," I complained.

"No, I guess not," Brenda said. "And even if we did, there's no stove, or kettle or anything."

"I bet you don't even have a cookie," I accused, hoping Brenda would at least look for one. She didn't.

"Sorry," said Brenda, biting her lip. "Mom just forgot, I guess. She's not taking this too well. It's…well…you know."

I didn't know and I wished people would quit saying that.

"Not even a marshmallow?" I suggested.

"I guess we'd better get going," Jennifer said. She seemed to be almost swallowing her words. Brenda nodded and they went to the back door.

"A cracker?" I asked hopefully. Jennifer pushed me out the back door. "Bye Brenda!" I yelled, and bounded down the steps. I was delighted to discover that the wind had gone down some and the snow was fatter and softer against my face. Maybe I wouldn't freeze to death after all.

Brenda and Jennifer were still saying good-bye so I ambled down the driveway watching the people coming and going from the front door. I spotted a lovely long stick leaning against a crumpled cardboard box and picked it up. I tested it on Brenda's fence. It made a delicious *acketty-acketty* sound as I ran it along the rungs. Jennifer caught up to me just as I passed my second fence.

"You're supposed to wait for me, Pip," she growled. "Boy! Wasn't that awful? It just wasn't Brenda's house anymore. It was *creepy.*"

Acketty-acketty-acketty went my stick. We crossed the street and except for the music of my stick we walked in silence back to the little store.

"No," said Jennifer when I suggested we go in. "We're late now."

"But I got a quarter!" I howled as she dragged me across the street.

"How can you possibly think of candy at a time like this?" she asked, choking a little.

"Are you crying, Jen?" I asked.

"Yah…I guess…it's….Oh, Pip! You just don't understand," she cried and began to sob.

"I'm sorry you're losing your best friend, Jennifer. Really," I said, resisting my stick with great difficulty.

"It's more than that, Pip! You just don't understand."

No, I did not understand. I felt small and stupid as I trudged along beside my big sister.

We crossed another street and were now walking alongside Mrs. Agatha Spencer's backyard which was surrounded by a perfectly splendid tall wooden fence, just right for my stick. I could not resist it and immediately began to run my stick along the pickets. *Acketty-acketty-acketty.* It was music to my ears. *Acketty-acketty-acketty.* I could hardly hear Jennifer crying it was so wonderfully loud. And apparently I did not hear the low warning growls of Spike who sat on the back porch of Mrs. Agatha Spencer's house. Nor did I see the Doberman, a moment later, slowly stand and stare at my small red figure which was coming ever closer.

Acketty-acketty-ack--. The stick stuck. I bent over and reached through the fence to un-stick it. What had it caught on? Somehow it had become wedged firmly between a snow-covered stone and the fence.

"Oh, Pip!" cried Jennifer, lifting her head and her voice to the sky. "Oh, Pip, it's so terrible! A true calamity!"

I dug away around my stick. It wouldn't budge.

"A tru-u-u-u-ue caa-a-a la-a-a mi teeee!" wailed Jennifer, her hand against her forehead.

A black form suddenly sailed off Mrs. Agatha Spencer's porch, hit the snow covered ground on the run and headed straight for my little blue mitten.

"Oh, Pip!" sobbed Jennifer. "We're going to lose *our home*, too!"

"*Aaaaaaaaah!*" I yelled as Spike's teeth sank into the tip of my mitten.

"*We'll be homeless waifs!*" shrieked Jennifer as I yanked backwards and tumbled onto the sidewalk in front of her.

"Are you teasing my poor doggy again?" Mrs. Agatha Spencer yelled as she came out onto her front porch. "You horrid children! I ought to report you!"

"What?" asked Jennifer, as I struggled shakily to my feet.

"You got his mitten, did you Spikey, Darling?" cooed the old lady as Spike pranced back to the porch, my blue mitten grasped firmly between his teeth. "Well, it serves you right, you little beast!" she yelled at me. "I hope you freeze your hand off."

"Did Spike just take your mitten?" asked Jennifer, looking bewildered. Still shaking, I could only nod. "You give back my brother's mitten!" yelled Jennifer.

"I most certainly will not," Mrs. Agatha Spencer yelled back. "Maybe it will teach him a lesson. It's a crime to tease poor dumb animals. He ought to be ashamed!"

"Oh, fudgie!" murmured Jennifer. "Come on, Pip. Put your hand in your pocket and let's get home. That old lady and her dog should both be locked up."

I followed Jennifer into the next yard and up the steps to our house. I waited, shivering, for Jennifer to unlock the door and then rushed into the welcoming warmth of our front hall.

Chapter Two

WHEN JENNIFER FOUND THE SOLUTION

"**M**y feet hurt," I complained as Jennifer helped me off with my boots.

"I'll get a towel and you can sit on the couch and rub them," Jennifer said.

I went into the living room and curled up on the couch. I was miserable.

"Well, take your socks off!" ordered Jennifer, coming in with the towel. I did and when I did there were two bright red feet staring up at us. "Fudgie!" exclaimed Jennifer, as she poked and prodded them. "Well, at least there aren't any white spots."

"White spots?" I asked, beginning to get a little nervous. With Jennifer, it was always best to be a little nervous.

"Brenda told me about them. White spots are frozen spots. If you get them you might have to have your feet cut off."

"*Cut off*!" I yelped. "What're you *talking* about?"

"Well, Brenda's cousin, who lives down the road from where she's moving to, got his feet frozen so badly they cut them off. Like this," she said as she raised her open hand and brought it down like a big axe across my ankles. "Chunk!" she said.

I jumped and began looking for white spots.

"Now rub your feet with the towel 'till they're warm," Jennifer ordered. She didn't have to tell me twice, believe me. "I'll go put a load of laundry in the washer." I was still rubbing frantically, my pulse throbbing, when she returned. "Pip, we gotta talk." I kept right on rubbing, the whole couch bouncing as I did. Nobody was going to cut my feet off! "Oh, stop it already," complained Jennifer. "You'll rub them right off."

"But what if they're *frozen*?" I cried, imagining that axe plunging down across my ankles. Oooooooo!

"Are you screaming in pain?" asked Jennifer, as she climbed up into the big chair opposite me.

"No," I said, still rubbing, ignoring my tired arms.

"Then they're not frozen."

"Oh." That did make sense, though one had to be careful with Jennifer. I dropped the towel and the normal colour began to return to my feet.

"Pip, I have to talk to you about Brenda. I have to explain."

"Yah, what?"

"Well, her parents had to sell their house and now they're moving away. And they didn't want to."

"Then why are they doing it?" I asked, taking another look at my feet just to make sure Jennifer wasn't lying.

"They *had* to," said Jennifer, in her *stricken* voice. "Her dad lost his job when the Plant closed and when they went to renew their mortgage the new payments were so high they couldn't pay them."

"What's a mortgage?" I asked, as I tried to see all the back of my heels.

"It's what you pay for your house. Payments. Like rent except when you finish you own your house."

"Oh," I said, not really listening. Was that a white spot or just where my thumb had pressed. It was hard not to scream, while I waited to see. Just my thumb. Whew!

"Anyway, now they're moving way out west to Brenda's grandma's," continued Jennifer. "And interest rates are so high that when our mortgage comes up for renewal we won't be able to pay it either! I just know it!"

I stopped looking at my feet and stared at Jennifer. Just *what* was she saying?

"And the mortgage is due for renewal this coming fall!"

"You mean we gotta leave our house...*my room...my BED...* this *fall*?"

"Oh, Pip, what'll we do?" cried Jennifer, throwing her arms over her face. "I can't bear to lose our house!"

I continued to stare at her. Lose our house? Sell my bed? I looked around the living room. It was cozy and warm and the furniture was old enough that Mom didn't mind if I put my feet up on it. Not like at Jeff's house. Not live here? Not have my bed? The yard? the big old oak tree out back? *"Jennifer!"* I wailed.

And that's when we heard the footsteps on the porch.

"Mom!" cried Jennifer. "Sssssh! Don't say anything, okay? Act normal."

Act normal? I was about to lose my only home, my only room and my only bed and I was supposed to act *normal*?

The front door opened and I heard my mother's cheery, "Hi Gang! I'm home!" It was too much. A sob escaped from somewhere deep inside me and I scrambled off the couch and rushed to the front hall and my mother's reassuring warmth.

"Pip, Dear, what's wrong?" she asked, hugging me. Oh, it felt so good. I buried my face in the folds of her dress. I felt very small. "What's happened? What's the matter?" my mother cried as she walked me back into the living room. "Jennifer, what's this all about?" she asked as she and I sat down on the couch, her arms still around me. I watched as Jennifer swallowed and swallowed again. What would she say? "Did something happen on the way home from school, Jennifer?"

"Uhm, yah," she said, a look of relief crossing her face. "That's right. We were going past Mrs. Agatha Spencer's and that Spike got Pip's mitten."

Right! I'd forgotten. But now that I remembered, I remembered the fear, too.

"Are you all right, Pip?" Mom cried and immediately began counting my fingers. "Well, they're all here anyway. I wish someone besides me would report that dog," she said. "No one believes me!" Then she noticed my bare feet. "Did you get your feet wet, too?" she asked.

"Just cold, Mom. Jennifer said they might *cut them off*!" I wailed. The dog! My feet! My house! My bed! They added up to a terrible wail and howl.

"Jennifer!" Mom scolded. "Cut off his feet! What a thing to tell him!"

"I didn't say he'd get *his* feet cut off, Mom. I just told him about Brenda's cousin. He's so *gullible*!"

"Well, that'll do it and you should know better. It's all right, Pip," Mom said, giving me an extra squeeze. "Brenda's cousin lives way out on the prairie. It gets much colder there than here. Your feet will not get cut off. I promise."

She wiped my tears away and I began to feel a little better. I sat back on the couch, relieved, and admired my wonderfully important feet.

"And speaking of Brenda, Jennifer," Mom said, "How are you?"

Brenda! *The house*! *My bed*! That's what I'd been crying about! I felt a sob trying to squeeze up from the very pit of my stomach. I scrambled off the couch and dashed out of the room and up the stairs to the safety of my bedroom.

"Put some warm socks on, Pip!" Mom called.

While tears trickled down my cheeks and my nose dripped into my drawer, I dug around for my skate socks. When I found them I sat down on my beloved bed and pulled them on. Alternately, I tugged on a sock and wiped my nose on a sleeve and hoped Jennifer could keep Mom downstairs until I could quit sniveling.

Socks on, I went over to the window and looked down on Chestnut Lane. It was home. All of it. Jeff lived across the street. I liked Jeff. Sometimes he babysat us and sometimes he let me watch him play hockey and sometimes he even played catch with me. I would miss Jeff when we moved away. And to where were we going to move, anyway? I began crying even harder and by the time I was all cried out and had washed the tears from my face, Mom was calling me for supper.

Jennifer glared menacingly at me when I entered the kitchen. "Keep your head down," she whispered. "Your eyes are all red and puffy."

I guess I did all right 'cause Mom never said anything about it. She was in too much of a hurry and finished eating almost before I started.

"Can you kids hold down the fort while I rush over to the garage?" she asked.

We nodded. "Why?" asked Jennifer.

"Because someone is coming over to look at the apartment and I need to turn up the heat and do a little dusting."

"Who, Mom?" I asked. I hoped it wasn't a girl like the last one.

"I don't really know myself, Pip," Mom said, gathering up her dishes. "It's a cousin of a girl I know from the office."

"Male or female?" asked Jennifer.

"A young man," Mom answered as she pulled on her boots.

I ate in silence while Mom was gone. I kept wondering what this person would be like. I had not liked the girl that had rented the apartment. She never spoke to me. Not once. I was glad when she moved away just before Christmas. Now someone new was coming. It seemed to me that it was enough having cranky old Mrs. Agatha Spencer and mean old Spike around without having someone living above our garage. It made me feel crowded and I didn't like it. Mom said the word was claustrophobic.

When I finished eating I helped Jennifer clear the table and stack the dishes next to the sink. Mom returned just as the phone rang.

"Will you get that, please, Pip?" she asked.

It was Wendy from next door.

"I just wanted to find out what your Mom's wearing tonight," Wendy said in her high little girl's voice.

"Whatcha wearing tonight, Mom?" I asked. "It's Wendy."

"Oh, how odd. Well, I plan to get into some jeans and a big sloppy sweater and relax," Mom answered as she undid her boots.

"Jeans," I said.

"Really?" asked Wendy. "I was planning to wear my brown tweed."

"Wendy's wearing her brown tweed," I relayed to Mom.

"That's nice. Is she going out?" Mom asked between puffs while she struggled with her boots.

"Goin' out?" I asked Wendy.

"Oh no! Has she forgotten the shower?" asked Wendy.

"You forget the shower, Mom?"

"The shower!" screeched Mom as the boot she was tugging on suddenly slipped off and she toppled over onto the counter. She straightened and rushed towards me and snatched the phone right out of my hand. "I forgot, I forgot!" she yelled as though Wendy had suddenly developed a loss of hearing. "Get off the phone! I've got to get a sitter." Mom jammed the receiver down and began dialing.

"Mom, I don't need a sitter. I'm old enough to baby sit."

"Maybe you are, Jennifer, but I'm not ready for you to be old enough. Not at night."

"Who you calling, Mom?" I asked.

"Lisa."

"I want Jeff."

"I want Lisa, but there's no answer. Friday night! I probably won't get anyone!" Mom dialed again.

"Who you calling now, Mom?" I asked.

"Joan."

"I want Jeff."

"I want Joan," said Mom. But Joan had already gone out for the evening.

"Jeff," she said before I could even ask.

"Yay!" I cheered. "I want Jeff!"

"I want anybody," Mom said as Jeff answered. "Well, Jennifer," she said after she'd hung up. "Jeff's coming so it'll be up to you to see that Pip brushes his teeth and gets to bed at a half decent hour."

"Okay, Mom."

"Well, I've got to rush. I wish I didn't have to go out tonight and leave you again, but Leslie is an old friend."

"It's all right, Mom," replied Jennifer. "We'll manage."

In other words Jennifer was going up to her room and listen to her music all evening.

"Well, it can't be helped." Mom got a box from the closet and set it on the table.

"What's that?" I asked.

"Leslie's present. A casserole dish." She got out the wrapping paper and a bow. I watched as Mom quickly cut and taped the paper in place, and slapped on a bow. "Now to get changed," she mumbled, and rushed out and up the stairs.

"Are you going to dry these or not?" grumbled Jennifer.

Actually, I hadn't even noticed that Jennifer had begun to wash the dishes. I picked up the tea towel just as the front door bell rang. I raced to the front hall and opened the door for Wendy.

"Wendy's here, Mom!" I screeched and ran back to the kitchen. In a moment Wendy swished in, wearing a dark red dress with long puffy sleeves.

"Hi, Sweeties!" she chirped and sat down at the table.

I dried a glass. The doorbell rang. I dashed off to answer it.

"Jeff's here!" I screeched above the sound of Jeff's blaster.

"I can tell!" Mom screeched back.

I watched Jeff in amazement as he took off his jacket and boots without once setting his blaster down or losing the beat.

"How ya doin' kid?" Jeff asked as he sauntered into the living room and sprawled on the couch, his blaster still attached to his ear.

"Pip!" yelled Jennifer from the vicinity of the sink. I raced back to the dishes.

Mom walked in wearing a navy pant suit. "Oh, Wendy!" she exclaimed. "I thought you were wearing your tweed pant suit."

"Well, I was, but the wind went down. It's really nice out now."

"I thought we were wearing similar things," grumbled Mom. "You're always doing this. Sometimes I wonder if you do it deliberately just to outshine me."

Wendy laughed. "Don't be silly, Susan." Then she winked at me. Did the wink mean she did do it on purpose? And what difference did it make, anyway? I'd have to remember to ask someone. Maybe Jeff would know. Nah.

"Listen, Wendy," Mom said. "I just have to explain this lease to Jeff and then I'll be ready. Thankfully it's perfectly straightforward. Even Jeff can't mess this up," she laughed and went into the living room and began shouting at Jeff to turn his music down. The music stopped and the house felt oddly empty.

"Lease?" asked Wendy. "You renting the apartment?"

"Yup," I answered, as I dried a pot. "To a guy."

"Oh?" asked Wendy, cocking her head, and straightening her shoulders. "So, who's the guy?"

"A cousin of a friend of Mom's" Jennifer answered. "Only maybe. He's coming to see it tonight."

"Is he, now?" asked Wendy. "Maybe I should stay and baby sit you guys instead of going to this shower."

"Jeff's sitting!" I cried.

"Hmmmm. Well, yes, I guess I have to go. A friend and all that. So is this guy a hunk with big bucks or what?"

"Dunno," I said, shrugging my shoulders.

"None of us have met him, not even Mom," supplied Jennifer.

"Well, whoever or whatever he is, I hope you rent it. Your Mom has notices on every bulletin board in town. She could really use the dough. Come to think of it if he had big bucks, he wouldn't be renting a little bachelor pad above your garage, now would he? Gee, I hope he's not too big a loser. Hope he can at least pay the rent. Don't suppose you can count on anything more than that, if that." She rolled her eyes. "Now, Leslie! She's the smart one!"

"Who's Leslie?" I asked.

"That's whose shower they're going to," growled Jennifer. "Can't you remember anything?" She turned to Wendy. "Why is Leslie so smart?"

"What's a shower?" I asked.

"Well, Sweetie, " said Wendy, ignoring me, "she is marrying a surgeon."

Jennifer drained the sinks and sat down across from Wendy. "And that makes her smart?" she asked.

"You bet it makes her smart, Sweetie. *Real smart*. She's *fixed for life* and you better believe it."

Mom came in and kissed us good night. "Now don't stay up too late, Pip," she said.

I nodded, knowing it didn't really matter. Jeff was sitting and I was confident Jeff couldn't even tell time.

We followed Mom and Wendy to the front door and Jennifer went out onto the porch.

"You'll freeze!" Mom warned her. "Get back inside."

"I thought you said you can only freeze where Brenda's moving, not here. You said, Mom!" I cried, visions of Jennifer having arms and legs cut off.

"And I meant it, Pip. It's just an expression. Honest."

"Yah, dummy," quipped Jennifer.

"Jennifer! What have I said about name calling?"

"Sorry, Mom. Sorry, Pip." She mumbled. "But, Mom, I really, really need to know something." Mom gave her one of her 'don't try me' looks and walked down the steps and out to the car, and Jennifer followed right behind. I went out onto the porch so I could be certain to hear everything. If no one was going to listen to me, I, at least, was going to listen to them.

"What's fixed mean?" Jennifer asked, and Wendy began laughing.

"Why, Jennifer," said Mom, "you know what fixed means. To have something repaired."

"No, I mean…uh…fixed for life. Like Leslie is because she's marrying a surgeon."

"What have you been filling these children's heads with now, Wendy?" laughed Mom.

"Just telling them the way it is."

"Well, I think what Wendy means, Jennifer, is that Leslie's husband-to-be earns a lot of money."

"He's rich?" asked Jennifer.

"Well, he certainly isn't hurting, Sweetie," laughed Wendy as she got into her car.

"Don't pay any attention to her, Jennifer," grinned Mom. "Leslie loves her surgeon and that is what is important."

"Hah!" screeched Wendy from her open window. "Don't you believe it!"

Mom got in next to Wendy and the car began to back out of the driveway. I watched the headlights flickering over the snow and bushes that grew along the fence that separated our property from Mrs. Agatha Spencer's. Then I saw him. A black skulking shadow out for his evening run. For a moment I couldn't speak. I couldn't think. I looked for Jennifer. She was just standing on the walk staring at the dark empty driveway. I found my voice.

"Jennifer!" I screamed. "Run! *It's Spike!*"

Jennifer saw him then and began to slowly back up towards the bottom step. Spike stood perfectly still watching her, his head down. A low growl crashed through the silence of the night.

"*RUN!*"

Jennifer turned and bounded up the steps as Spike leapt through the air and landed with all four feet running. One, two, three steps and Jennifer was at the top. I held the door as she ran inside. As I was pulling the door shut I saw Spike, fangs bared, land on the porch. At that moment Jennifer yanked me inside by my shirt. I heard the fabric rip and saw Spike's feet touch down on the mat in front of the door. Spike's head slammed into the glass door. He backed up, shaking his head and ambled off towards home.

My legs were shaking so hard I had to sit down on the stairs.

"Oh, Pip!" exclaimed Jennifer. "Isn't it great?"

"Huh?" I asked. I was examining my ripped shirt. Ruined. First my mitten, now my shirt, and in between those, my feet and bed and all in one day!

"We're saved! We're saved!" cried Jennifer.

"Yah, but it was a close call. He almost got us."

"Who?"

"What do ya mean, who? *Spike!*"

"Oh, yah, that," said Jennifer.

"*That!* Look at my shirt!"

"Oh, never mind your old shirt! Our house is saved!"

"It is?" I couldn't quite see how Spike nearly eating us for lunch had saved our house. But I knew better than to say so to Jennifer.

"Don't you see?" I shook my head. I felt small and stupid again. "But didn't you hear? Leslie's fixed for life."

"So?" Now I knew I was stupid.

"*Think*, Pip," cried Jennifer. "All we have to do is find a rich husband for Mom. Then we won't have to worry about the mortgage." She began dancing around and around. "We'll have scads of money! *We'll be fixed for life!*"

I stared into her laughing, excited face. "*What?*"

"We just have to find a rich husband for Mom!" Jennifer repeated. "Simple!"

"*Just?*" I asked. Somehow that didn't sound so simple.

Chapter Three

WHEN JENNIFER STAYED IN HER ROOM

Jeff still had his blaster wrapped around him when we went into the living room. He hadn't noticed the commotion with Spike. I switched on the television.

"What's on?" he asked.

"Space Wars."

"All *right*!" He turned his music down a decibel. "You got good taste, kid."

"Pip," growled Jennifer, switching the set off. "This is not the time to be watching TV."

"Hey, kid, what gives here?" asked Jeff, actually sitting up.

"Yah!" I echoed. "What gives?"

"We have serious matters to discuss, Jeff, and they're none of your business."

"Then go discuss somewhere else. I'm watching Space Wars."

Jennifer switched on the TV. "Okay. Come on, Pip."

"But that's not fair! I wanna watch, too."

Jennifer grabbed my hand and began tugging. I screeched at the top of my lungs. Space Wars was one of my top twenty favourites.

Jeff turned his blaster off. "Get off his case, all right? He wants to watch Space Wars and that's *my* business."

"But it's important, Jeff!" she whined.

"Will it still be important in an hour?" he asked.

"Of course."

"Then let the kid watch now and discuss later."

Jennifer stomped out of the room and I curled up on the couch next to Jeff. The action was just getting exciting when we heard a car screech to a stop outside. I looked out the window and saw a small red sports car under the street lamp in front of the house. The person inside unrolled the window, stuck his head out and then glanced at a paper he held in his hand. Seemingly satisfied he jammed the car into reverse, darted backwards a few yards and then roared into the driveway and slammed to a stop.

"Must be the cousin guy," I said.

"What cousin guy?" asked Jeff.

"About the apartment," I said, getting off the couch.

"Apartment?"

"He's coming to see the garage apartment. Don't you remember? You're supposed to show it to him. Mom gave you the lease didn't she? And the key?"

"Oh, yah, yah, the lease. Sure kid. Let's go." Jeff clambered off the couch and followed me to the door. We got there in time to see a tall, thin man unfold out of the little red car.

"Maybe I should go get Jennifer," I suggested.

"Nah! Leave her alone to sulk. She's too annoying. We can handle this."

I grinned. For once I was going to be in on something that Jennifer missed out on. We both had our jackets and boots on by the time the man had taken in his surroundings and mounted the steps.

"I...uh...came to see the...uh...apartment," the man said as Jeff opened the door.

"Right," said Jeff, sauntering out with me at his heels.

The man immediately grasped my hand and shook it. "Hi there...uh...fella. My...uh...name's Harry. What's yours?"

I was so taken aback that for a moment I just stared up at that smiling face. "It's...Philip."

"How do you...uh...do Philip," Harry said. "Glad to meet you."

"But everyone calls me Pip," I said, grinning.

"Then Pip it...uh... is," said Harry

"That's Jeff. He lives over there," I said, pointing to the house across the street.

"But you...uh...live here?" asked Harry. I nodded. "Good!"

I smiled again. I liked this Harry person, I decided, as we made our way to the garage and up the stairs to the small apartment. Jeff switched on the lights and Harry glanced at the kitchenette, peeked in at the bathroom and then stood in the center of the only other room. He paced off the length and width and then turned to Jeff.

"Okay," he said.

"Okay, what?" asked Jeff.

"Okay," Harry repeated. "I'll...uh...take it."

I jumped up and down, I was so excited. "Oh, wow! You're really going to live here? Really? Really? Really?"

"Yah. Is that...uh...okay?"

"Wow! Is it! Wait'll I tell Jen!"

"Jen?"

"Jennifer. My big sister."

"Another kid? Uh...good. My lucky day."

I know I beamed. It was certainly my lucky day. This Harry person had already said forty-one words to me and that was forty-one more that that lady who used to live here had ever said to me.

"You...uh...like cats?" Harry asked.

Forty-four words! Wow! "Yah," I said. "We used to have a cat."

"Good. I have...uh...one."

"Really? Will you let me come pet him sometimes?"

"All you…uh…want, Pip."

"What's his name?"

"Fluffy."

Wow oh wow! Boy oh boy! This was my very luckiest day! A little fluffy cat and a man who talked to me. If we had to rent an apartment in our garage, then this was the guy I wanted in it. I could hardly wait until I told Jennifer.

I watched excitedly as Harry signed the lease in the kitchen and gave Jeff a cheque. I watched as Harry went down the steps. I watched as he folded himself up again and got back in his little red car. And I watched as Harry roared out of our driveway and across the street into Jeff's driveway, slammed on his brakes and roared forward and away. Then I raced up the stairs to Jennifer's room.

"Jennifer!" I screeched, running in and flopping onto her bed. Jennifer was sitting at her desk with a pen and notebook in front of her, her radio blaring. "Jennifer, he's taking the apartment!"

"The cousin person?" she asked and shut off the radio.

"Yah. His name's Harry and he talked to me and everything."

"Oh, goody," she said, but I could tell she didn't mean it.

"Really. He shook my hand and everything. You missed out on the whole thing," I gloated. I was going to make the most of this, 'cause she was always gloating about something to me.

"You should have called me when he got here, Pip. Does he have any money? Can he afford to pay the rent?"

"How should I know? I guess so. He gave Jeff a cheque and signed the lease and everything."

Jennifer gave me that 'you're so little and stupid look'. "Really? It's all done and you never even called me."

I was beginning to worry. What if the guy couldn't pay his rent. Maybe that's why he was being so nice. "Yah, well, sorry. But, he's moving in first thing in the morning."

"What's he look like?"

"Tall. Real skinny. I dunno."

"What'd he have on?"

"Aw, Jen, I can't remember everything. What difference does it make?"

"*Tell me!*" she commanded.

"Uh, he had a jacket on."

"Well, I should hope. It's January. What was it like?"

"Uh…it had a pocket."

"Just one?" asked Jennifer crinkling her forehead.

"The other one was there, but it was just sort of hanging."

Jennifer sighed. "Uh huh. Go on."

"And his socks were blue I think."

"You saw his *socks*?"

"Well, see, they were sort of stuck out of his sneakers."

"You mean his pants were too short?"

"Noooo. I don't think so." I was really getting nervous, now.

"Then what do you mean?"

"Uhm, well, see, a couple of his toes stuck out of his sneakers. And I think he had blue socks on."

"Oh, brother, wouldn't you know it!" groaned Jennifer.

"Unless that was the paint and the socks were red," I said, struggling to remember.

"Paint?" asked Jennifer.

"His sneakers were sort of covered in paint. Kind of." Did paint somehow make this still worse?

"And holes?"

"Yah."

"*Wouldn't you know it!*" Jennifer repeated.

"Know what?" I asked, afraid to hear the answer.

"He's broke."

"What do you mean? How do you know?"

"Obviously, he's dirt poor, or he wouldn't have come looking like that with holes in his shoes and ripped pockets and stuff. And paint all over."

"Just his shoes. I think."

"When you go looking at an apartment or anything, you try to look your best, so the landlady will think you're okay. But if this is his best, Pip, then he's dirt poor. And besides, it's the middle of winter. You don't go around wearing holey sneakers in January unless you can't afford boots."

My heart sank. "Well, I don't care if he is poor. I like him."

"Honestly, Pip, don't you ever think? What has liking got to do with anything? Liking someone doesn't get the rent paid. He'll always be behind in the rent and then one day he'll simply take off owing us scads of money. Don't you know anything?"

"Aw, Jen, you don't even know him." I started for the door.

"Hey, where are you going?"

"To my room," I mumbled.

"Pip! We've got a lot to discuss."

"About what?" I was not in a good mood. What if she was right about Harry?

Jennifer sighed again. "About our new father, what do you think?"

"New *father*?"

"Honestly, Pip! Can't you remember anything for more than two minutes? We're going to find Mom a rich husband and when they get married that'll make him our step-father."

"Oh," I said. I really wasn't certain this was a good idea, but I followed her onto the bed and curled up next to her. She propped a notebook up against her knees and put the end of the pen in her mouth like she always did when she was thinking big thoughts.

"He has a cat named Fluffy," I said.

"*Fluffy*? How original."

"Yah, and I'm allowed to pet it."

"Now," declared Jennifer, ignoring me, "the first thing we have to do is decide on what we want, 'cause we don't want a man like Mr. Henderson for a dad."

"No!" I shrieked, horrified at the very thought.

"Well, let's start with him and what we *don't* like."

I thought for a minute. Mr. Henderson was our principal and just the mention of his name made me feel sick to my stomach. "He scares me," I said.

"Okay," said Jennifer. "Under the Unwanted list I'll write 'scary'. What else?"

"Well, he makes us sit at our desk with our hands in our lap until school starts. He won't let us talk or play a game or anything. And even when he lets us go on a field trip we aren't allowed to talk and when I asked him a question at the museum he made me go out and sit in the bus."

"So that takes care of 'mean', 'ignorant', and 'dictator'."

"What's a dictator?" I asked.

"Somebody who has to be the boss all the time and order everybody else around. A control freak who thinks he's right all the time. And in this case an adult chauvinist pig."

"What's that?" I asked, beginning to feel small and stupid again.

"Somebody who thinks kids don't have any rights."

"Oh," I said, thinking that that described most adults. We added a few more things to the list like 'yelling' and then Jennifer started the Wanted list.

"Rich," she said, writing it down and adding 'poor' to the unwanted list. "What else? That about covers it for me."

I thought about Harry. "Someone who likes kids."

Jennifer wrote that down and added 'generous' to that list and 'skinflint' to the unwanted list. "Doesn't do us any good if he has money but won't spend it on us. I need a scooter and more music and of course more Barbie stuff."

"More Barbie stuff! It's me that needs stuff! I need tons of Lego!"

"Yah, yah. Whatever."

I thought of Jeff. "Oh, definitely someone who plays ball with me and soccer and stuff. Hey! Let's find a baseball player for Mom!"

"He'd be rich all right," mused Jennifer, pen in mouth. "but I don't know how we'd get one."

"We could write a letter to one."

"Hmmmm. Maybe."

"Could we, Jen? Could we?"

"No, I don't think it's a good idea."

"*Why?*" I screeched. "Why can't I have the father I want? You always get everything *you* want."

"I do not! And anyway it's not like we're going out and buying him like a toy or something. It's gotta be somebody Mom's going to like, too."

"And who says she won't like a baseball player, anyway?"

"Well, I've been thinking," said Jennifer. "I think a baseball player would be macho and Mom doesn't go for macho."

"What's macho?"

"Thinking that he's a big strong man and that that's all that's important in life."

"Oh. What else is?" I asked. I wanted to be a big strong man almost more than anything else.

"Being generous and nice and good," declared Jennifer. "And being a woman."

"How about a hockey player?"

"Same thing."

"Oh."

"Anyway, we need to come up with names of prospective rich fathers. Who makes a lot of money?"

"Mr. Henderson?"

"Nope. Not enough. We're not settling for middle-class, here, Pip. We're going for upper-middle-class at the very least." I didn't understand and said so. "More money, more everything. Doctors, for instance. Even better, a specialist. Like a brain surgeon."

"Ooooo. Yuck!" I groaned. The image of my new father cutting up brains and coming home with some still stuck on his hands grossed me out.

Jennifer turned the page in her notebook and made a new heading entitled 'profession' and wrote down 'doctors' and under that she wrote 'psychiatrists' and 'brain surgeon'. "I know! A pediatrician!" shrieked Jennifer. "It would be perfect! He'd have scads of money and he'd *have* to like kids." She wrote that down and made a giant star beside it. "Tomorrow we'll get out the phone book and get some actual names. It's going to be tricky finding out who's married and who isn't. It's going to be even trickier getting him to meet Mom."

"Are you sure we should do this, Jen?" I asked.

"Do you have a better idea to save our home?"

"No."

"Okay, then, be quiet. And I really mean *be quiet*. Don't you dare breath a word of this to *anyone. If you do, your life will not be worth living!*"

And I knew that was true! Just then I heard a car turn into our driveway. "Harry's back!" I squealed and jumped off the bed and raced down the stairs. Jeff was still watching television.

"Jeff!" I yelled. "Harry's back!"

Jeff slowly sat up and just as he did, the doorbell rang.

"Come on! It's Harry!"

"So, answer the door, kid," Jeff mumbled.

I opened the door, but Harry wasn't standing there. It was a young man in a gray overcoat with a white shirt and tie showing.

"Pardon me, but is your mother in?" asked the man.

"Jeff!" I screamed. "It's not Harry!"

The man stepped inside and closed the door. I stared at him and the man stared at the ceiling. After a few moments Jeff ambled in.

"I'm here about the apartment," the young man said. "Are you in charge?"

"The apartment?" asked Jeff, as if in a fog.

"*The apartment?*" asked Jennifer.

I turned around. Jennifer was standing on the landing looking down, her eyes as big as silver dollars.

"I was told by my cousin—"

"*Your cousin?*" shrieked Jennifer from above.

The man glanced up at Jennifer then back at Jeff. "I was told by my cousin that you had an apartment for rent. I had an appointment to see it this evening."

I looked at Jeff. Jeff looked at me.

"Oops," said Jeff.

Chapter Four

WHEN JENNIFER MET HARRY

The day dawned crisp and clear, the snow dazzlingly bright beneath the winter sun. But towards noon it began to cloud over and the occasional snowflake was seen drifting down. By noon it was definitely snowing.

"I thought you said he'd be moving in this morning," Mom said, sipping her lunchtime coffee.

"That's what he said," I replied, taking another bite of my sandwich. I was feeling very blue. Harry had run out on us before he'd even moved in.

"I hope he's as nice as Marion says he is," Mom said. "Most young men like to party a lot and have girls over and heaven knows what. What did he look like Jennifer?"

"I didn't see him. Just Pip and Jeff." Jennifer looked down at the floor. My sandwich stuck on the way down.

"Oh, dear. Well, what did he seem like, to you, Pip?" she asked.

"He's really nice, Mom. And he's old like you, but not like Mrs. Agatha Spencer."

"Like me? I thought Marion said her cousin was only twenty. You probably just thought he was older because he had a business suit on."

Jennifer hid her face in her notebook.

"Well…" I stammered, "he…um…well…no…but he has a cat, Mom."

"Oh? Maybe he's a lot more mature than most twenty year olds then." Mom liked cats and tended to judge people's characters by how they behaved towards cats. "A cat. That's nice." She finished her coffee and began clearing the table.

"Mom, who makes a lot of money?" asked Jennifer.

"My boss."

"Lawyers?"

"Yes. Definitely Lawyers."

Jennifer wrote 'lawyers' in her notebook. "Who else?"

"Mmmmm. Let's see. Doctors, lawyers, top executives, some businessmen, and real estate agents if the economy is on the upswing. Like that. Professionals."

Jennifer was writing madly. "I don't want any 'ifs', Mom. I want sure things."

"What's this for?"

"A school project. Who else?"

"Odd project. Dentists."

"Dentists?" asked Jennifer. "Who else?"

"Oh, I don't—" Mom stopped and whirled around as we heard the screeching of tires and a loud crash. We ran to the front door.

"Good heavens!" cried Mom when she opened the door and we looked out. There was Harry's red sport's car crumpled up against the big Maple tree at the corner of our driveway.

I felt myself beaming. Harry had arrived!

"Uh…How do…uh…you do?" asked Harry as we rushed over to the car. "I'm…uh…Harry Cunningham."

"Are you all right?" cried Mom. "Should I call an ambulance?"

"No, no. A…uh…tow truck, perhaps." Harry opened the door and unfolded himself.

"Here, please let me help you," Mom said. She took Harry's arm and they walked up the sidewalk to the front door.

"I hope you're not going to tell me this is *our* Harry," whispered Jennifer.

I nodded happily and reached inside the car for the huge black fluffy cat. "Wow!" I gasped. "You're big!" Under Fluffy's weight I struggled up the drive to the house.

"*Our Harry?*" Jennifer repeated.

"Yah!" I cried. "And this is Fluffy!"

"You gotta be kidding! You two morons rented our apartment to *this*?"

"Fluffy!" cried Harry, turning around.

"It's okay. I got him," I said. Fluffy purred contentedly in my arms as we followed Mom and Harry into the kitchen. Mom called a tow truck while I got down a bowl and poured some milk for Fluffy. He lapped it up and then wrapped himself around my legs asking for more. I happily obliged.

When Mom got off the phone she made some hot chocolate for Harry. "It'll help calm your nerves," she said. "Can I get you anything else?"

"Yes, thank you," said Harry and Mom made him a tuna sandwich. I set the almost full can down on the floor for Fluffy.

"Mom!" cried Jennifer, pointing at me and the can. Mom scowled at me. Fluffy devoured the tuna as quickly as Harry devoured his sandwich.

"More?" asked Mom, sounding a little nervous. Harry thanked her and she got out another can and made two sandwiches and put the rest of the tuna in the fridge. Fluffy was purring around my legs, asking for more. Mom bent down to pet him.

"What a beautiful cat!" she exclaimed, reaching out her hand. All in a split second Fluffy's back went up, he hissed and snarled, and his fully armed claw slashed the air.

Mom jumped back. "Pip!" she gasped. "Stay away from him!"

"Oh he…uh…loves children," said Harry.

"Better let him have the tuna, Mom," Jennifer suggested.

Mom nodded and took another step backwards. Jennifer retrieved the tuna and set it down for the now purring Fluffy.

"Would you like a piece of pie?" Mom asked as Harry devoured his third sandwich.

"Lovely," said Harry as a small moving van backed into the driveway, edging it's way around Harry's crumpled car.

"We've just rented our apartment," Mom explained as she cut a piece of raisin pie for Harry. "I guess his things have arrived." She handed Harry the pie and went out to unlock the apartment for the movers.

We watched as the movers carried in a bed, and a big upholstered beat up old chair.

"The…uh…chair's Fluffy's," Harry told us.

Then the movers carried in a big desk.

"That's mine," he said.

Then a high stool, two large shelving units, and a peculiar looking table were carried out of the truck.

"An artist's desk," Harry explained. "It tips up and down. It's…uh…mine."

"Well, that explains the paint," Jennifer said, looking down at Harry's sneakers. "Probably the holes, too."

Then several huge roles of paper went in and a few boxes. I saw Mom talking to the movers and waving her arms around. She finally turned and came running back in. I fervently hoped she was not rushing in to kill me.

"I don't know what's going on," she gasped as she pulled her boots off. "Those can't be the belongings of an insurance salesman." Boots off, she began paging through the telephone book.

"Mom," said Jennifer. "There's something you should know."

"Not now, Dear. I have to phone Marion."

"But Mom, this is Harry."

I wondered if, perhaps, now would be a good time to disappear.

"Dear, please," said Mom. "I have to call Marion. I think there's been a mistake." She dialed the number.

Harry was looking at the pie again. I cut each of us a piece and began to edge past Jennifer in hopes of making a safe retreat to my bedroom. But you can't put anything over on Jennifer. She clamped her hands onto my shoulders and held tight.

"But, Mom," whined Jennifer. "Harry is the one—"

"Ssssh," whispered Mom. "It's ringing….Hello, Marion. Susan, here. I was calling about…But I…Well, I wasn't home and…I'm sorry, Marion, I didn't know, I…Yes…Honestly. There's been some sort of mistake and…Yes…Good-bye." She hung up and went into the dining room.

"There's been a mistake," Mom said, grabbing the lease from the table. "I can't quite make out this signature. Harvey? Henry? Harry? Something. Last name starts with a C, I think. Pip you'd better tell me more about this person, whoever he is."

Jennifer's claws dug more deeply into my shoulders. It was really very difficult to swallow the pie.

"Mom," said Jennifer. "This is Harry Cunningham." She pointed dramatically at Harry who was eating his pie with obvious enjoyment.

"Yes, I know, Dear. Now who do you suppose—" Mom suddenly stopped and stared at the tall, thin, ragged man who was devouring her pie. "Harry?" she asked, her voice sounding weak and frail.

Harry nodded.

"*You're* renting our apartment?" she asked.

Harry nodded again, smiled, and swallowed the last bite of his pie.

Mom slumped into a chair. "And you don't have a cousin named Marion?" she asked.

"No. Should I…uh…have?"

"Probably," said Mom. I thought Mom looked a little tired all of a sudden. "Well, it's signed so I guess there's nothing can be done about it," Mom mumbled. "I don't suppose, Mr. Cunningham, that you'd consider moving out?"

"Move out?" gasped Harry. "But I…uh…just moved in, Mrs. Miller. And I…uh…well I like it here."

"No doubt," said Mom, glancing at the empty pie plate.

Harry looked around the kitchen. "Or did you mean …uh… move in here?"

Surprisingly, Jennifer jumped at the idea. "Great!" she cried. "Then we'd have money from a boarder, too." Mom shook her head violently. "But, Mom! We need the money!"

"Not *that* badly!"

"And then Fluffy could sleep with me!" I cried.

"No, no, no, *no!*" screeched Mom. "It just wouldn't be proper, that's all." And the idea was dropped. Rather heavily, I thought, the way Mom glared at us. I was very sorry that it was, for the idea of having a cat cuddled up beside me in bed had been a perfectly delicious one, and it was hard to let the idea go.

I decided to spend the afternoon holding Fluffy and watching Harry get settled. However, watching Harry get settled didn't take very long. He set up his bed in one corner and placed the big chair in front of the window.

"Fluffy likes to…uh…look out the window," he said.

I sat down in it, and Fluffy curled up on my knee. Then Harry placed his desk next to the bed and set his artists table in the middle of the room. Along another wall he set up his book shelves and began unpacking boxes of books. I decided to help.

"Hey, how come you got so many kids books?" I asked, looking through the boxes.

"I…uh…like them."

"Why?" It seemed odd for an old person.

"To study."

"You *study* kids books?"

Harry slid another box over to me. "Uh...look in there."

I opened the box and began looking through the books. "Hey! I got this one. And this. And, hey, here's my favourite one!" I smiled at Harry. "You like the same books as me."

"What's this...uh...say?" he asked, pointing at the words along the bottom of one of the book covers.

"Story and Pictures," I read, "by Harrison J. Cunningham." Harry nodded. "Hey, his name is almost the same as yours."

"Harry can be...uh...be a nickname for Harrison," said Harry.

"Oh," I said. "Then he's got the same name as you. Maybe. What's your second name?"

"James."

"Wow!"

"It...uh...is me, Pip."

I stared at him. *"Really?"* He nodded. *"Really and truly?"*

"It's my job to...uh...study kids books. And kids."

"Are you going to study me?" I asked.

"If it's...uh... okay with you."

"I guess so. I've never been studied before. Is it hard to make books?"

"Well, it's the only thing I'm any...uh...good at. Plumbing... uh...would be much too difficult."

I spent the rest of the afternoon convincing Jennifer that it was true and persuading her to go and see for herself.

Jennifer looked through the books. "Gee! Here're some of mine, too. You write books for my age, too?" Harry nodded. "Can I bring some kids over to meet you?" she asked.

Harry nodded.

"He studies kids," I informed her.

"Oh. Well, I don't know if they'd want to be studied," Jennifer said. "How do you study them?"

"I…uh…guess you could say I'm…uh…studying some right now."

"You are?" asked Jennifer, looking around.

"He means us," I said, feeling especially good that suddenly I knew things Jennifer didn't.

Jennifer laughed. "Well, I guess that'd be okay, then. Do you make much money?"

"I don't know. Does it…uh…matter?" asked Harry.

"Of course it matters," said Jennifer. "But I guess it was a stupid question," she said as she looked around the sparsely furnished apartment, and then back to the shabbily dressed Harry. "Too bad you don't."

"I don't understand," said Harry.

"Never mind. School project."

Harry laughed and Jennifer blushed. I realized he didn't believe her and wondered how he knew.

"Everyone's work is…uh…important, Jennifer," Harry declared. "Unless it's…uh…illegal, but that's not really work, is it?"

"Yah, but some people's work is more important than others."

"Whose?" asked Harry.

"Doctors," Jennifer stated, with hands on hips. "They save lives."

"Uh…yes," agreed Harry. "But so do firemen, policemen and lifeguards."

Jennifer sighed, and rolled her eyes. "That's different."

"Not if…uh…you're the one drowning, or trapped in a…uh…burning building."

I giggled. I couldn't help it. Jennifer scowled at me.

"But doctors keep you from getting sick, too," she said.

So do farmers and…uh….garbage men."

"*What?*" cried Jennifer, throwing up her arms. "That's crazy!"

"Is it?" asked Harry. "If there were no farmers then there'd be… uh…no food. Then you'd…uh…be worse than sick. You'd be dead."

"Yah, but—"

And if our garbage wasn't disposed of, it'd pile up and pile up and before…uh…long…well.…germs and all that. Rats. Plagues. Again, dead."

"Oooooooooo," shivered Jennifer. "So who makes a lot of money?"

Harry thought a moment. "Mobsters," he said. "And…uh… drug dealers."

Jennifer scrunched up her face. "We gotta go for supper," she said, and stomped out.

"What're you having for supper, Harry?" I asked.

Harry scratched his head. "I don't know. I think I…uh…forgot to get groceries."

"*You forgot?*" I cried. I couldn't imagine forgetting food. Harry nodded and began placing his books on the top shelf.

"You don't have *anything*?" I asked.

"I don't know," said Harry. He began to rummage through his remaining boxes. In the box of underwear and socks he found cat food, cereal and crackers. "There!" he cried *holding* up the cereal and crackers as if it was a trophy.

"That's your *supper*?"

"Well, I don't seem to…uh…have anything else," said Harry. He set the boxes on the desk and went back to his bookshelves as if it didn't matter.

"I could get you something," I volunteered. "The corner store doesn't close until eight o'clock."

Harry rummaged around in his pockets until he found a badly crumpled five dollar bill and I set off for the store with the bill tucked inside my mitten.

Jennifer was waiting for me at the foot of the stairs, and decided to go along. "That's probably all the money he has," she said, shaking her head.

"Don't be long," Mom called after she'd given permission for us to go. "Supper is nearly ready."

"Can you fake a tooth ache?" Jennifer asked me as we crunched our way along the snow covered sidewalk.

"Dunno. Why?"

"Well, try it." I groaned and held my cheek. "Not bad. With a little practice you could probably get away with it."

"Why do you want me to have a toothache?" I asked. I kicked a lump of snow out of my path. It broke into a zillion pieces and scattered all along the sidewalk.

"I don't want you to have a *real* toothache. Just a pretend one."

I skrinkled up my nose. I did not like the sound of this. "Why?" I asked, not at all certain I wanted to hear the answer.

"I've been thinking. Mom said dentists make a lot of money."

"So?"

"So our dentist is a bachelor. Well, he used to be married but he isn't anymore."

"So what?"

"So that makes him a good candidate."

"For what?" I asked, kicking another lump of snow.

"Oh, Pip!" she sighed. "Don't you ever pay attention to anything? One: he makes a lot of money. Two: he isn't married. That makes him a perfect candidate for our new father."

"*What*!" I screeched. "A *dentist? Yuck!*"

"Yes. A dentist," declared Jennifer as she opened the door of the store.

I was certain I had a real toothache all the way home with Harry's hot dogs.

Chapter Five

WHEN JENNIFER TOOK PIP TO THE DENTIST

I had practiced having a toothache so many times for two weeks that I began to think I really did have a bad tooth.

"Okay," said Jennifer, coming out of the kitchen. "I phoned Mom and she's going to phone Dr. Wiggins and then meet us there, so come on."

It was a beautiful Friday afternoon in early February. The sun was shining and the snow had all melted. It felt like spring. As we walked down the steps we saw Harry drive past in his beat up sports car.

"Guess he forgot where we live again," Jennifer said, snickering.

"He doesn't *forget*," I declared. "He's just busy thinking about something else, that's all."

"Mmmhmmmm," agreed Jennifer, but I could tell she didn't agree at all.

"Don't you like him?" I asked.

"What difference does that make? It's totally irrelevant."

"What's that mean?"

"It means Harry doesn't matter. Our problem is saving the house and whether or not I like Harry doesn't matter one way or the other."

"Well, it matters to me!" I cried.

"Okay, Pip. He's great. He's wonderful."

"But Jen, he is!"

Jennifer sighed one of her long sighs. "It's just that he's so hopeless. Harry never knows where he is or what he's doing."

"He does so!" I screeched. Defending Harry was becoming a full time job. "See? Here he comes back again."

"Well, what choice did he have, Pip? This is a dead end street."

I planted myself by our driveway and waved in a pointing fashion so that Harry could not help but see the driveway. The thought of Harry driving around until he ran out of gas again was too much. Once was embarrassing enough.

"Hi, Pip," Harry called as he slammed on his brakes. "What're you…uh…doing here?"

"Going to the—"

"Just going to meet Mom," interrupted Jennifer.

"Want a…uh…lift?"

"No!" exclaimed Jennifer. "Pip just *loves* to ride the bus."

"Sure?" asked Harry.

Jennifer poked me in the ribs. "Yah. Sure," I said, and then, much to my embarrassment, Harry continued down the road.

"Told you!" gloated Jennifer. "He forgot where he lives again!"

"You don't know that!" I cried. "Maybe he's going somewhere. And why couldn't we have gone with him anyway?"

"Really, Pip. One: Harry is a crazy driver and we'd probably have an accident and not get to the dentist's at all. Two: If Harry didn't have an accident he'd get lost as usual and again we wouldn't get there. Three: You'd have to fake a toothache all the way there instead of just after we get there."

I had to agree and we proceeded to the corner to wait for the bus.

"Got your token ready?"

I began to dig in my pockets when I heard a low growl. The hair stood up on the back of my neck. Spike! He was sitting on the front step of Mrs. Agatha Spencer's house. Then I saw the cat.

"Fluffy!" I screamed.

Fluffy was walking very slowly across Spike's yard. He seemed to be completely unaware of Spike's presence though he was only a few feet from the porch. Was Fluffy deaf?

"Fluffy!" I screamed again, and Jennifer, too, began calling frantically. But Fluffy sat down and began washing his face.

"Fudgie! That crazy cat is just like his owner," growled Jennifer. "He's a regular nutso."

Suddenly Spike leapt off the porch and at that exact same moment Fluffy took off, fairly flying across the yard towards us. Just inches from the fence Spike pounced, all fangs bared. We held our breath, knowing poor Fluffy was a goner. But Fluffy sprang straight up and Spike smashed with a dizzying scrunch into the fence. Fluffy hopped up onto the railing, then down onto the sidewalk. With tail and head held high he strutted past us and into our yard.

"You kids hurting my little Spikey again?" shrieked Mrs. Agatha Spencer from an upstairs window.

Spike was still standing in front of the fence, shaking his head.

"No," Jennifer called, "we didn't do anything." We looked at each other and burst out laughing.

"I know you did, you little fiends!" she screamed above the whine of the bus as it braked next to us.

"I can't find my token," I cried. But Jennifer was too busy laughing to get mad. She dug another one out for me and waved to Mrs. Agatha Spencer as the bus pulled away from the curb.

"Now, you remember what you're supposed to say and do once we get there?" Jennifer asked.

"Yah," I said, but I was getting a little nervous. As much as we'd rehearsed this little scene, I was still afraid Jennifer would really get mad if I blew it. Then I saw Harry's car pass us, go through a red light up ahead and turn, with screeching tires to the right. Traffic slammed on their brakes. Horns honked. Harry disappeared around the corner.

"What an airhead!" cried Jennifer. "He's lost again, and if anyone ever asks, we *do not* know him."

"He is not lost!" I cried in defense. "He's thinking!"

"You're as hopeless as he is!"

"Am not! I mean—"

"Forget it! Let's run over all the possibilities again."

Twenty minutes later we were outside the dentist's office and I went into my act. I put my hand over my cheek and groaned. Jennifer opened the door and we went in.

"Oh Pip!" cried Mom, getting up from a chair. "How is it, Dear?" I groaned. "Oh, my goodness. Well, it won't be much longer now. Dr. Wiggins will see you right away."

The dental assistant took my hand and led me into one of the patient's rooms and helped me into the chair. Mom was right behind.

"No!" shrieked Jennifer. We'd forgotten Mom would come, too!

"It's okay, Mom," I gulped. "I don't need you here."

"You don't?" she asked. She looked just like she had when I'd accidentally hit her in the stomach with my football last summer.

"He's too big for that, Mom," Jennifer said.

"Well, if you think," she muttered. I nodded. "If you change your mind, Pip, I'm in the waiting room."

A few minutes after they left, Dr. Wiggins came in. I was beginning to worry that he'd get mad when he discovered there was no toothache.

"Well, young man," he chirped. "I hear you have a terrible toothache." I nodded. "Open wide and let's have a look see."

"It feels okay now. Maybe I don't really have a bad tooth. Maybe it's something else."

"Well, it won't hurt to have a look, now, will it?" he said, and stuck a mirror in my mouth. "Mmmmm. Mmmmmm. They're pretty small. I'm surprised they caused you any pain at all."

"What?" I gurgled.

"Two small cavities in the same tooth, Philip. But we'll soon have them fixed up."

"*Now?*" I cried. "But I don't really have a toothache. It's all a—"

"Well, Philip, a lot of people say that as soon as they get to the dentist's the toothache disappears. However, I'm afraid if you go home without getting it fixed, the pain will return. And this being Friday, you'd have to suffer all weekend. So let's get right at it, shall we?"

I wanted to call Mom, but I knew Jennifer would kill me if I did. I dug my toes into my shoes as the needle went into my gum. Just wait'll I get hold of Jennifer. This was *not* part of the deal. How come I was in here suffering while she was out there reading comics? I fumed and plotted to get even while my nose and tongue went fuzzy. I'd put salt in her cereal and a dead mouse in her drawer. I'd—

"Well, how's it feel now, Philip?" asked Dr. Wiggins. "Pain all gone?" I nodded. "Excellent. Let's get to work shall we? Open wide."

I opened wide and listened to the whine of the drill and hated Jennifer. At long last the dentist took his hands out of my mouth and announced the job was done. The lady took off my bib and removed the suction tube. I was about to get out of the chair when I suddenly remembered my mission. Jen really would kill me if I forgot. Now what was it I was supposed to say? *I couldn't remember*!

"Uh. We're probably having fried chicken for supper tomorrow," I blurted. What would the dentist do? Would he realize the truth now? And be terribly angry?

"That's fine, Philip," Dr. Wiggins said. "Eat something soft for supper tonight and by this time tomorrow, you'll be able to eat anything."

"Oh. Okay." Now what? What was I supposed to say? The dentist wasn't supposed to say *that*! What? What? "Uh...do you like fried chicken?"

"Love it!" said Dr. Wiggins. "One of my favourite foods." He helped me out of the chair, put his arm around me and walked me to the door.

"Uh. Well it's at five o'clock. You'd better wear a tie, though, 'cause Jen says I have to." Was that it? I didn't think so. What? We were going *through* the door now. What? What?

"Pardon?" asked Dr. Wiggins.

"At five o'clock. We'll see you at five for fried chicken. Tomorrow," Then I saw Mom and Jen. Jen was looking peculiar. Like she'd swallowed a worm. "Mom!" I cried. "Dr. Wiggins is coming for supper tomorrow at five. I told him we'd have fried chicken. Come on."

"Hurry up, Mom," Jennifer said, and grabbed Mom's hand. I thought Jen's face looked awfully pink. Like she was too hot or something.

"Supper?" asked Dr. Wiggins. "I'm invited?"

"At five," said Jennifer.

"Fried chicken?" asked Mom.

"My favourite," said Dr. Wiggins.

"Well, then, we'll see you at five, I guess," mumbled Mom. She was shaking her head and looking like she does when she first wakes up.

"Wow!" whispered Jen as we walked out to the bus stop. "It worked! It really worked! I'm a genius! And it was easy as pie."

"*Easy*!" I cried. "I had two cavities filled!"

"Gee! Good thing we went, Pip. You might have gotten a toothache."

I hit her. She yelled.

"Pip!" cried Mom. Why did you hit Jennifer?"

"I got two fillings! And I hated it! I hate having somebody's hands in my mouth!"

"Pip, for goodness sakes! You should be thanking Jennifer for bringing you to the dentist. It's not her fault you had a toothache. Now apologize."

"Yah," said Jennifer. "Apologize."

"I'm sorry," I mumbled. I wondered where I could get a mouse. Maybe from Fluffy. Maybe two mice.

"That's okay, Pip," said Jennifer. "I understand. Pain makes us do strange things."

I scrunched my hands into my pockets to keep from hitting her again.

"That's very mature of you, Jennifer," Mom said, as we boarded the bus to go home.

I had to clench my fists, scrinch my face up, and push down hard on my toes to keep from tripping Jen as we walked down the aisle to our seats.

The bus was crowded with people going home from work and we all had to sit in different places. All I could do to Jennifer was occasionally try to stick out my numb tongue at her. The effect seemed to lack something and I gave it up to watch the buildings and traffic go by. I saw Harry pass us again. *He really was lost*! I hoped Jennifer hadn't seen him. I'd never hear the end of it, if she had.

Chapter Six

WHEN JENNIFER SLEPT

Home from the dentist's, we were immediately busy getting supper on the table and laundry underway. I had no opportunity to tell Jennifer off. The numbness in my mouth was beginning to fade, but my anger was not.

Mom had dished up the macaroni and cheese and the hot dogs before she even noticed Jennifer was not at the table. "Jennifer!" she called. "Where are you? We're waiting supper."

I heard the freezer lid in the back porch close and a moment later Jennifer came in.

"What were you doing?" Mom asked. I thought Mom had been strangely quiet since we'd gotten home.

"Just checking," Jennifer said.

"Checking what?" Mom asked.

"Chicken," said Jennifer.

"Chicken?" asked Mom. "Oh. Yes. Chicken. I simply don't understand it.

I've been going to him for years and never has he ever....Do we have any chicken?" Jennifer nodded. "Enough?"

"Yes. Two. Better cook them both, Mom. Men eat a lot and Dr. Wiggins is a big man."

"Uh huh. Sure. I don't understand this at all! Just what did he *say*, Pip?"

"Who?" I'd been playing with my still slightly fuzzy tongue.

"Dr. Wiggins! About *supper*!"

I didn't know what to say. Jennifer hadn't told me this part. So I just shrugged.

"Well, how did it come about? What did you say? What did he say?"

I began squirming. "Uh…well…he asked me what we were eating. He said I shouldn't eat any hard foods tonight. And I said we were having fried chicken tomorrow." I stuffed the last half of my hotdog into my mouth so I wouldn't have to say anything else, but with the freezing not all the way out yet, I didn't know if I was going to choke to death or spit it all out on the table. Mom didn't even seem to notice.

"Well?"

"Whoumph?" I asked through the hotdog. Wasn't she always telling me not to talk with my mouth full?

"*What did he say next*?" she asked. A little too loudly, I thought. This was all Jennifer's fault.

"Then," said Jennifer, as she gave me a swift kick under the table, "he said fried chicken was his favourite food and he sure wished he could come. So what else could Pip do, Mom, but invite him. Pip told me all about it." I nodded enthusiastically. "Personally, I think Dr. Wiggins has the hots for you."

"*Jennifer*!" screeched Mom. "Wherever do you get these expressions from?"

"Wendy."

"Then stop talking to Wendy." We ate in silence for a while, then Mom asked, "Do you really think so? I mean that he's got the…well, that he likes me?"

"Oh, sure!" exclaimed Jennifer. "Why else would he invite himself over?" She winked at me.

I stuck my tongue out at her. My jaw was beginning to ache from having those big fingers stuck in my mouth for so long.

"Well," said Mom, grinning in a funny way. "Who would have guessed? Of course he has been divorced for quite a while now."

"Oh, a long time, Mom."

"Maybe you're right, Jennifer," said Mom and then she *giggled*. Like Jennifer!

"*Probably* I'm right," said Jennifer, beginning to giggle, too.

"What are you talking about?" I asked.

"Nothing, Dear. Just girl talk," Mom said, then turned back to Jennifer. "Now what should we have besides chicken?"

"Something that's good for teeth," said Jennifer and they both laughed.

I groaned and left. There was nothing funny about this. If Mom married a dentist we'd always be eating stuff that was good for teeth. *And I'd never see another candy as long as I lived*! And every time I got into trouble I'd get sent to the *dentist*!

I turned on the television but it was still too early for Space Wars, so I laid on the couch and imagined how awful life would be if Mom married our dentist. And that night I thought about it in bed. Every time I shut my eyes I could see Dr. Wiggins coming through our front door and Jennifer throwing her arms around him and calling him 'Daddy'. And Dr. Wiggins smiling and giving her *another* Barbie doll to add to the pile of Barbie dolls that totally filled the living room. And then Dr. Wiggins *would reach out to me, and stick his big fingers in my mouth*!

It was no use. I couldn't sleep. I crawled out of bed and went into my sister's room. I still hadn't told her off.

She was sitting up in bed, reading. "Pip, you were terrific!" she cried when she saw me.

"I was?" This wasn't what I expected.

"The best! I wasn't sure it would work, but you pulled it off! You were *brilliant*!" Wow! Brilliant. Me! "I'm so proud of you!"

"You are?"

"Of course I am! You're the best little brother a girl could have!"

"I am?"

"And I'm *so sorry* about your fillings!"

"Oh. Yah. That. That's okay." For some reason I wasn't angry anymore.

"And it's all going so well," sighed Jennifer. "I've talked Mom into wearing her red dress. I noticed Dr. Wiggins had a red tie on, so he must like red." How does she notice stuff like that? "And Mom seems excited about the dinner party. And Pip, we have to clean the house up. It's gotta be spotless!"

"Why?"

"He's a *dentist*. Just think, Pip. A dentist for a father! Won't it be wonderful!"

"No desserts!" I groaned. "And he'll probably have to practice on us on weekends."

"Oh, Pip! You get the silliest ideas."

"He'll always have his fingers in our mouths."

Jennifer laughed. "Don't be silly, Pip. He's just like anybody else when he's not at work. Does Mom type at home all the time?" I shook my head. "Well, dentists don't dentist at home either."

"You sure?"

"Of course I'm sure. And just think of all it will mean. A car of our own. Vacations. Loads of stuff at Christmas and birthdays."

"Really, Jen?"

"Of course! I asked Wendy the other day and she said Dr. Wiggins is loaded."

"Maybe I should ask him just to make sure."

"*NO!* Don't say anything about money, Pip, or he'll think we just want him for his money."

"Don't we?"

"Well, yah, mostly, but he's got to be nice, too."

"Hey, you two," said Mom, coming into the room. "Get to sleep. It's late."

But I still couldn't sleep. I kept thinking of all the aspects of my life and how a dentist in the house would change them. Mostly I wondered if a dentist would ever play ball with me. I'd have to ask Jen if it was okay to ask him that. I hoped he wouldn't say it was too dangerous because I could get all my teeth knocked out. And hockey, too.

At last I heard Mom come up the stairs and get ready for bed. I listened to all the sounds and tried to guess what she was doing, but I could only be sure of the brushing the teeth part. She tiptoed in and kissed me on the cheek. I pretended to be asleep.

Finally, the house was still and I sneaked out into the hall. Mom's light was still on. She must be reading in bed. It made me feel better. Somehow I didn't want to be the only one in the house awake. I crawled back into bed, turned my light on, and began to make a list of all the things I'd like Dr. Wiggins to get me. Maybe they'd be married by September. My birthday was in September.

A sound! *Footsteps*! I sat up. The footsteps were on our front walk. Now they were on our porch! I slowly got out of bed and crept to the window. I gently pulled back the curtain and peered down. I gasped in terror, dropped the curtain and ran into Mom's now darkened room.

"Sssssh!" cautioned Mom who was standing by her window.

"There's someone on our step, Mom!" I whispered. "Who is it?"

"I don't know," Mom whispered back. She put her arms around me and held me close, but I was still terrified. "Pip, go back to your room. Hide in the closet and don't make a sound until I come for you. Understand?"

"But I want to stay with you!"

"No argument, Pip. I have to get to the phone quickly and call the police. Now do as you're told."

I tiptoed back to my room and listened to the very noisy burglar trying to open the door.

"Hey! Anybody home?" called the burglar, knocking loudly.

Laughing, I ran downstairs and opened the door for Harry.

"Sorry officer," I heard Mom say. "It's a friend."

"What's going on?" asked Harry, looking a little bewildered. "Don't you people answer the doorbell anymore?"

I tried the doorbell. "Doorbell's broken, Mom," I called as Harry and I walked into the kitchen. Mom was sitting at the table with her head in her arms.

"Mom!" I cried. "Look! It's Harry!"

"Harry, I should kill you!" cried Mom, and she burst into tears.

"What's wrong? What'd I do?"

"I thought you were *a burglar*! Or worse!"

"A burglar? *Me*? Uh...why?"

"WHY? What did you expect me to think when I saw a man on my doorstep, in the middle of the night, trying to get the door open?"

"You ...uh...didn't answer your doorbell," said Harry. "You might have been...uh...hurt."

"Or we might have been asleep!" cried Mom, wiping her eyes.

"Is it that late?" asked Harry.

"I repeat," said Mom. *"It's the middle of the night!"*

"Oh. Well...uh...that explains why the corner store is...uh...closed."

Mom sighed. She looked awfully tired. "Can't you afford a watch, Harry?"

"I dunno. I'll have to see. How much do they...uh...cost?" he asked.

"Twenty dollars and up," answered Mom.

Harry dug around in his pockets and pulled out two twenty dollar bills. "Guess so. You...uh...think I should buy one?"

"Yes, Harry, you should definitely buy one," Mom said. "And when you have it, you should definitely look at it once in awhile."

"I'll...uh...try to remember. Now that I think of it...uh...well... my last landlady said that too. And a calendar."

"Oh, my goodness," groaned Mom and she began rubbing her forehead.

Harry rushed over and began pressing a spot on each side of her head with his thumbs.

"*What are you doing?*" exclaimed Mom.

"Uh...well...getting rid of your...uh...headache. Better?"

"A bit. Yes." Mom sounded surprised. Harry moved his thumbs to the base of her neck "It's gone!" cried Mom, a moment later. "Where'd you learn that?"

"Dunno. Somewhere." Harry went over to the fridge and looked in. "Got any food I can...uh...buy?" he asked.

"Is *that* what you're here for?" asked Mom.

"Yah, I think I...uh...forgot to well, to eat today," he said, pulling a frankfurter out of the fridge and eating it. "And then I couldn't find a grocery...uh...store."

"*You forgot to eat?*" I shrieked.

"Can't be sure," said Harry. "I seem to...uh...recall eating a cheese...uh...sandwich. I just don't remember when."

"I made you a cheese sandwich yesterday after school," I said.

"Yah, that's it," said Harry, beginning to rummage through the fridge again.

"But that was almost a day and a half ago, gasped Mom.

"Well, it came...uh...back," mumbled Harry from inside the fridge.

"What came back?" I asked.

"Hunger," Harry said, as he emerged with a salami. "It does that. Rather a nuisance, but there you have it. Anybody want some…uh… salami?" He ripped off a hunk and began eating.

"Are you telling me," asked Mom, "that you have not eaten anything since Pip made you that cheese sandwich?"

"Dunno," said Harry, taking a piece of cheese. "Don't recall. I've been…uh…busy."

"Don't you have any food over there?"

"I told you he didn't, Mom," I said.

"But he must eat *something*!" cried Mom.

"I went to…uh…MacDonald's," Harry said as he swallowed the last of his salami and cheese. "But…uh…they were closed, too." He dug around in the fridge some more and finally emerged with a bowl of macaroni and a bottle of ketchup.

"You're so thin!" cried Mom.

"Am I?" asked Harry. He sat down at the table across from me and dumped half the bottle of ketchup on his macaroni. "Uh… fork?" I got him a fork and Harry began to wolf down the cold macaroni.

"Is your door unlocked?" Mom asked. Harry nodded, and Mom went out, carrying a flashlight. In a few minutes she returned and slumped into a chair. "You really don't have any food over there. Can't you afford to eat?"

"Oh, I…uh…think so. My accountant would have told me if I…uh…couldn't."

"*Your accountant!*" gasped Mom.

Harry nodded, finished his macaroni and went back to the fridge. I get…uh…busy. Involved. I forget."

"You forget!" I cried. I just couldn't imagine forgetting to eat, but then Mom reminded me how many times I'd been late for supper because I forgot.

"If you can afford an accountant, you can afford to eat," Mom said. "From now on you can have your suppers with us and I will do your shopping for you when I do ours. It'll cost you extra but at least you won't die of malnutrition."

Harry nodded and opened a jar of peanut butter and began making a sandwich. "Any...uh...jam?" he asked going back to the fridge.

"Is Harry really going to eat with us *every* night?" I asked. Mom nodded. Wow! Harry eating supper with us every night! "Can Fluffy come, too?" No one answered.

"You'll also need a watch so you can be here on time," Mom told Harry. "One with an alarm."

Harry nodded as he spread jam and mustard on the second slice of bread and placed it on top of the first.

"Shall I get you the watch?" Mom asked, "Or can you do that much?"

"You...uh...better," said Harry, as he took a bite. "I might... uh...forget."

I watched in amazement as Harry chewed and swallowed the amazing concoction. "Is it good that way?" I asked.

"Not really," Harry said. "It needs some...uh...pickles."

Chapter Seven

WHEN JENNIFER'S PLANS WENT AMISS

Saturday was a cloudy, damp day, with the fog rolling in off the sea and settling on the land. It shifted and danced its slow weaving dance along the roadways and buildings. I loved to walk through the field and down into the ravine behind the house in a heavy fog. It took little effort to imagine all sorts of eerie things. But today I couldn't go. Jennifer would not allow it.

"Pip!" she yelled from the foot of the stairs.

"Coming!" I tore myself away from the back window, gathered up the garbage bags and clumped down the stairs. Today, Jennifer said, was Father's Day. Today we would be having supper for the first time with our new father. It was a day to remember for all time, she said, and therefore everything must be perfect. "I don't see why we have to clean the upstairs," I grumbled, when I reached the bottom. "He's not moving in today, is he?"

"You never know," said Jennifer. "We have to be prepared. Anyway, the bathroom's up there and we don't want him to see a messy bedroom, do we?"

"We could close the doors," I mumbled. Jennifer just rolled her eyes at me and stomped into the living room. I hauled the garbage to the back door where I found Mom busy in the kitchen baking pies.

"What kind are you making, Mom?" I asked.

"Blueberry."

"Do dentists eat desserts?"

"Oh, Pip!" she laughed. Then she gasped. "Goodness! Maybe they don't. If I've gone to all this work for nothing…"

"Harry and I will eat them. Can I have a taste?"

"Pip, just take out the garbage, please." I headed for the back door. "I just don't understand any of this," she said. "It's him that has the money, and it's me that's footing the bill. And doing the work. And making dessert he won't eat."

I gulped and shut the door. I didn't think Jennifer was quite right when she said Mom was enthusiastic about the dinner party. I went around behind the porch, lifted the lid of the garbage bin, and placed the bags in it.

"Hi ya, Gorgeous!"

I jumped. I hadn't seen Wendy standing on her walk.

"Whatcha doin', Big Boy?" she asked as she came over to the fence.

"Nothin'," I said. I hated it when Wendy talked like that.

"Now, don't tell me nothing's going on. More than the usual Saturday chores, by the look and sound."

I nodded. "Company's coming for supper."

"Oh? Who?"

"Dr. Wiggins."

"Your *dentist*! You don't say. And not a word to me! Well, isn't your mother the sly one. I wonder how long this has been going on."

"*Nothin's* going on!" I screeched. "He's just coming to supper 'cause I invited him, that's all."

"*You* invited him?"

"Yah. So there!" I yelled, and turned back towards the house.

"Hmmm. How odd," Wendy said.

Inside, again, I saw the pies were safely in the oven, Mom was polishing the silverware, and Jennifer was polishing the dining room table.

"It's so long since I've used this set," Mom said to me, "that it's a wonder it hasn't tarnished itself to death by now. I almost wish it had."

But Jennifer heard. "Oh, Mom, it'll be great having real silver on the table and the good china and everything."

"Yes, Jennifer, and I'm just thrilled to be doing all this instead of relaxing on my day off."

"I knew you would be!" chirped Jennifer. Mom rolled her eyes at me again, and grinned.

"Pip, get out the vacuum!" Jennifer ordered.

"I already vacuumed!"

"Well, it's not good enough. Do the front hall and the living room again."

"Mom! Do I have to?"

"I don't know, Pip," sighed Mom. "I don't seem to know anything today."

"Well, I do know," said Jennifer. "I saw *a dust bunny!*"

"Oh, dear heaven!" exclaimed Mom. "The next thing you know, we'll see some lint and there goes the neighborhood."

"It's not funny, Mom!" said Jennifer. "Dentists are *CLEAN!*"

"Yes, you're right, Jennifer."

"See, Pip? Now get the vacuum!"

I got the vacuum. But I was getting a bit sick of all this. For two weeks I'd practiced having a toothache. Then I'd had *two* fillings. And now, all day, ever since I'd opened my eyes, I'd done nothing but work, work, work! I certainly hoped I wouldn't have to spend all my Saturdays like this after Dr. Wiggins became my dad. No amount of Lego was worth that!

By the time I'd put the vacuum away for the *second* time Mom had finished the silverware and was preparing the sauce for the veggies. I found Jennifer in the living room going through a bunch of CDs.

"What do you think?" she asked. "Modern or classical?" I shrugged. "I think classical. That should impress him. Make him think we're sophisticated."

"What's soph--. Never mind," I sighed. I didn't really want to know.

Jennifer put most of the CDs back in the drawer, but placed some on the stand next to the portable stereo. She looked at her watch. "Time to get dressed, Pip."

She dragged me upstairs and forced me into a blazer and tie.

"But this is for Sunday School!" I bellowed.

"Don't be such a baby. It is also for dinner parties." She stood back and took a long, scowling look at me, then readjusted my tie and ran a comb through my hair. "You'll do," she declared. "Now go downstairs, sit on the couch and *don't* move."

"Jennifer!" I wailed.

"You can't get dirty!" she ordered, glaring menacingly at me. "This is too important for you to mess up. Now go! I have to get ready."

I went downstairs and sat. And sat. And sat. It was worse than waiting at the doctor's office. It was as bad as, as bad as, well...Yes! It was as bad as waiting at the *dentist's* office.

I could smell the chicken, now, and even the vegetables in their sauce. I got so hungry, I was in agony. At last Jennifer came down, wearing her emerald green dress and black shoes that Gram had sent her for Christmas.

"Come on!" she called, and led me into the dining room where Mom was setting the table. "We'll finish that, Mom. You go get dressed."

"Well, well, well!" exclaimed Mom. "Don't you two look wonderful!"

Jennifer smiled and blinked her eyelids. I scowled. My tie was choking me. Now I wouldn't be able to swallow the chicken. Or the pie.

"You going to wear your red dress, Mom?" Jennifer asked.

"Well, I suppose I'll have to if you two are going to be so elegant. I was planning to wear my pant suit."

"Oh, no, Mom!" exclaimed Jennifer. "Your red dress is more appropriate." She blinked her eyes some more. What was that about, anyway? "Go. We'll finish the table."

"Well, if you're sure."

"Certainly."

"*Certainly?*" I asked, when Mom was gone. "*Appropriate? Soph… soph-whatever?*"

"Just practicing, Pip."

"For what?"

"To impress my new Daddy-kins."

I groaned. "And I don't think Mom wanted to wear her red dress like you said she did."

"Well, she's wearing it, isn't she? So she must want to."

"Yah, but not until—"

"Ssssh. She might hear you. Come on, we've got work to do. Put these paper serviettes away and I'll dig out the cloth napkins. And then look for the candles in the china cabinet."

I hurried and by the time I found the candles Jennifer had the napkins rolled up and inserted into silver rings beside each plate.

"Gosh!" I exclaimed. "Where'd you get those?" I reached out to touch one of the glistening rings.

"*Don't touch!*" squealed Jennifer. "You might smudge them!"

"Where'd you get them?" I repeated.

"Oh, Mom's got loads of beautiful stuff stashed away. Stuff she never uses. But I remembered them and I knew where they were."

She said it as though that made her some kind of hero or something.

I watched as she sifted through another drawer and came up with two beautiful glass candleholders. The cut glass sparkled in the light from the newly cleaned chandelier. I handed her the box of candles and she placed one in each of three holes in each of the holders and set them at an even distance from each other and the plates. She even got out a ruler! Then she dug around some more and brought out a long brass box and set it in front of one of the plates.

"What's that?" I asked.

"Matches," said Jennifer. "Long ones. For the candles."

I nodded and smiled. I couldn't help it. It was beautiful. All of it. Right down to the matches. I wondered what other treasures might be hidden around the house.

A car drove into the driveway. I looked at the clock. It was exactly five o'clock.

"He's here, Mom!" Jennifer called.

"I'm almost ready," Mom called back. "Oh, dear, *why* are we doing this, anyway?"

"See," said Jennifer. "She's so excited, she's confused."

Somehow, I didn't think that was the problem.

The doorbell rang and Jennifer opened the door with a flourish. Was that a little bow she gave as she ushered him in?

"Welcome," she said, in her sweetest voice.

"Well, thank you, Jennifer," Dr. Wiggins said. He stepped inside and removed his overshoes, then set a parcel down in the corner. A gift, maybe?

"Pip will take those," Jennifer said, motioning to the boots and giving me that 'ordering' look which I knew so well.

"Why can't he—" I began.

"PIP!"

I jumped forward, took the boots and placed them in the closet. Surely a grown man could have done that, I thought, but no, there was Jennifer taking his coat and smiling broadly as her eyes took in his brown tweed suit, cream coloured shirt and striped tie. She nodded her approval and then gave me that 'I told you' look which I also knew very well.

"Well now, young man," said Dr. Wiggins, coming towards me. I stepped backwards and smashed into the closet door. "Come now, I simply want to see how those teeth are doing. Open wide."

"See Jennifer! He does do that!" I cried, in alarm.

"Pip!" she growled through clenched teeth. "Behave."

I opened wide. Dr. Wiggins stuck his fingers in. And his fingers still smelled like they did in his office!

"Well," said Dr. Wiggins. "Those teeth look just fine. However, I can see that you've eaten since you last brushed your teeth." He wagged his finger at me.

"Just one cookie!" I cried. I had a strong desire to hit Jennifer again.

"Just one cookie!" cried Dr. Wiggins. "My, my! How often I've heard that! Well, Philip, in the first place you shouldn't eat cookies. And in the second place, it takes just one speck of food to start a cavity. Now run along and brush your teeth. There, now," he said, ruffling my hair. "There's a good boy. Better brush your hair, too, while you're there."

"Boys will be boys," sang Jennifer as she smiled sweetly at Dr. Wiggins.

I glared at Jennifer. This was her choice for a *father*? I vowed right then and there to write a letter to a baseball player and ask him to marry my mother. Better yet, I'd pretend to be my mother and sign her name. That would fix Jennifer!

Jennifer glared back, so I started up the stairs. As I reached the middle step, Mom came out of her room and started down. I stopped and stared. Mom was beautiful. Really and truly beautiful!

"Good evening, Dr. Wiggins," Mom said. Even her voice was beautiful!

"Good evening, Susan. And do call me Charles," Dr. Wiggins said, his voice all gaspy and his face glowing almost as much as the silverware.

"Come, Pip," said Mom as she met me on the stairs. "Time for supper."

"*Dinner*," whispered Jennifer, again through clenched teeth.

I followed Mom down the stairs. Dr. Wiggins was looking at Mom the way I supposed I looked at the Christmas turkey. I didn't like him doing that!

"I brought a little something, Susan," Dr. Wiggins said, and picked up the parcel from the corner and handed it to her. It was wine. "I thought it might enhance the chicken." He put his hand on Mom's arm.

"Why, that's lovely, thank you," said Mom and she led him into the living room.

"I'll get the wine glasses," Jennifer said, and scooted out of the room.

Dr. Wiggins was still holding onto Mom's arm.

"Just make yourself comfortable and I'll dish up supper," Mom said.

But Dr. Wiggins was clearly not about to let go of her. He stood there holding her arm and looking at her in that Christmas turkey sort of way. And I didn't like it! And I didn't think Mom did, either. She looked kind of squeamish, so I pushed my way in between them until he had to let go of her.

"When's supper, Mom?" I asked.

She gave me a big smile and a squeeze. "In just a minute, Pip. It's all ready."

"Are the children eating *with* us?" asked Dr. Wiggins.

"Of course they're eating with us." Mom said it a little snippily, I thought. "They *live* here."

"Well, yes, of course they live here, Susan, dear. It's just that I somehow expected—"

"Them to eat outside in the cold and the dark?" asked Mom. She was definitely snippy now.

"No, no," laughed Dr. Wiggins. "I just thought maybe they'd be at a friend's house, that's all."

"I hardly think so, Dr. Wiggins," Mom said, smiling in that weird way she had when I felt she wasn't really smiling at all. "They did half the work."

"Oh, did they? Well, isn't that nice. Uh, Susan, do call me Charles."

"Certainly, Dr. Wiggins," said Mom, and she left to dish up supper.

I stayed in the living room to stare at Dr. Wiggins. He looked so different without his whites on and without his fingers in my mouth. In a few minutes Mom called us for supper and I led the way down the hall to the dining room. We met Jennifer on her way to the living room. "Be right back," she said.

Now, as we entered the dining room, I saw that two long stemmed glasses had been added to the table and Dr. Wiggins's wine was placed beside his plate.

"Lovely!" exclaimed Dr. Wiggins. "Perfectly lovely! As you are, dear Susan."

"Candles?" asked Mom. "Where'd they come from?" Her red cheeks made her look embarrassed. "The…uhm…uh…children set the table while I was getting dressed," she stuttered.

"Of course they did," chuckled Dr. Wiggins, as though he didn't believe her. He picked up the wine bottle and with something of a flourish he popped the cork, poured a small amount into his glass, sniffed it, tasted it, and said, "Lovely! Perfectly lovely!" and then filled both glasses. "To you, Susan," he said, and took a drink.

I thought it was very bad mannered of him to take the first taste, and especially to *sniff* it, but I managed not to say it out loud.

Just as Dr. Wiggins was helping Mom, unnecessarily, into her chair, the music of Tchaikovsky resounded with a boom through the house. Mom nearly fell out of her chair. A moment later, Jennifer bounded in.

"Perhaps the Bach recording would be better suited to mealtime, Jennifer," Mom suggested, and Jennifer bounded out again. A moment later, a softer sound enfolded us and Jennifer bounded back in and took her seat across from me.

The food had just nicely made its rounds, and I was just beginning to enjoy the crunchy goodness of the chicken when we heard the back door squeak open and Harry call, "Am I late? I don't seem to have a watch yet."

Mom and Jennifer seemed to freeze in mid-bite.

"Oh, dear," said Mom, apologetically. "I totally forgot about last night." She got up and got another plate down from the china cabinet, set it next to me, then hurried out.

"*Last night?*" asked Jennifer, looking at me with dark, accusing eyes. "What about *last night?*" She was back to growling between clenched teeth.

"Harry's going to eat his suppers with us now," I informed her, excitedly.

Jennifer turned a sickly shade of greenish-white. "Harry?" she gasped. "*Harry? You could have TOLD me!*"

"Forgot."

"And who is Harry?" asked Dr. Wiggins.

"He lives in our garage," I said.

"He what?"

"He rents an apartment from us," explained Jennifer. Her face was all blotchy red.

"You have an apartment?"

"Well, Mom kind of dabbles in real estate, you know."

"Does she now? That's very interesting. I'll have to discuss it with her. I've stuck to stocks and bonds, but I've been considering other avenues."

"Well, yes, it's good to diversify."

Diversify? Dabble in real estate? What was Jennifer talking about?

Mom returned, with Harry at her heels. She moved me closer to her, and put Harry next to me, and kitty-corner to Dr. Wiggins.

Jennifer gasped. So did Dr. Wiggins.

"*What is this?*" demanded Dr. Wiggins, glaring at Mom.

"Hi kids!" said Harry, running a hand through his uncombed hair. He had obviously just crawled out of bed.

"This is my tenant. He's going to eat some of his meals with us. Dr. Wiggins, I'd like you to meet Mr. Harry Cunningham," said Mom. "Harry, this is our dentist, Dr. Charles Wiggins."

"Hi...uh...Doc," said Harry. Dr. Wiggins said nothing. He just glared. First at Mom, then at Harry.

"Harry!" whispered Jennifer. "You should have dressed."

"But I'm...uh...dressed," he said, glancing down at his scruffy paint splattered shirt and faded, torn jeans. "Pass the...uh... chicken...uh...please."

Jennifer seemed to squinch into her chair as Mom, smiling, passed the chicken to Harry.

Just as Harry was cutting his meat, Fluffy jumped onto his shoulder and reached a paw down towards Harry's plate. Harry handed him a bit of chicken which the cat devoured with relish. Then Fluffy, reaching for more, began to purr loudly. Dr. Wiggins stared at Fluffy with obvious horror, and Jennifer squinched so much she was in danger of disappearing beneath the table. As Fluffy devoured his third piece of chicken, Dr. Wiggins seemed to find his voice again.

"A cat!" he cried. "*A cat at the table!*" He reached over and tried to push Fluffy off Harry's shoulder. But Fluffy, growling and spitting, met the outstretched hand with his own outstretched claws. As Fluffy's claws dug into Dr. Wiggins's hand, Dr. Wiggins jumped up, swearing, and banged his knees against the table. The wine tipped over and ran across the table and onto Dr. Wiggins's pants. "Now look what you've done, you fool!" cried Dr. Wiggins. "My hands are my living! And this is a thousand dollar suit!"

Dr. Wiggins reached towards Fluffy again, this time with his fist. With a great yowl, Fluffy leapt. He landed right on top of Dr. Wiggins's head. As Dr. Wiggins's screams erupted, his fist landed right on Harry's jaw. Harry yelled and clutched his face. Fluffy dug his claws deeper into Dr. Wiggins's scalp, then jumped down to the floor.

Dr. Wiggins rubbed his scalp frantically with one hand, picked up his plate with the other, and dumped it, creamy vegetables and all, right on Harry's head.

"*STOP IT!*" shrieked Mom as the two men grabbed fistfuls of food and flung them at each other.

"Take…uh…uh…uh…*that*," Harry hollered as the salad flew.

"You disgusting vermin!" shouted Dr. Wiggins as another fistful of vegetables splattered across the floor.

"You revolting…uh…uh…*snob*!" screamed Harry as the mashed potatoes slopped over the dentist.

"*Guttersnipe!*" screamed Dr. Wiggins.

"*STOP IT! STOP IT! STOP IT!*" screamed Mom and Jennifer together.

I shuddered and scurried beneath the table for safety. Fluffy was already there, chewing contentedly on a piece of chicken.

Chapter Eight

WHEN JENNIFER SCHEMED AGAIN

One day in late February, I awoke to a blizzard that kept everyone at home. No school for Jennifer and me. No work for Mom. It was wonderful!

I spent the morning making a list of both ball players and hockey players I might like to have as a father. This was no easy task. After two hours of long, hard thinking I had narrowed my list to twenty-seven. I had just begun to wonder what to write in my letter when the power went off, making it an even more wonderful day.

Harry and Fluffy had to seek refuge in front of our fireplace with the rest of us. We played games, told ghost stories, and sung songs. We had candles and an oil lamp for light and for supper we had a wienie roast. I was certain it was the very best day I'd ever had in my entire life!

The power came back on just before bedtime and the blizzard stopped around noon the next day, not in time for the roads to be cleared for school or work.

I went out the back door, wearing my snowsuit, mittens, boots, and scarf and stood there, staring at the biggest, firmest, snowdrift I'd ever seen! It was so high it reached almost all the way up to

Harry's landing. There was nothing else to do but build a snow house. And a magnificent snow house it would be!

I plowed waist deep through the snow to the garage door and found my shovel. I decided the entrance to my house could not be at the front for everyone to see. No. This would not simply be a house. It would be a secret hideout!

I plodded through the snow to the back of the garage and the drift. Here there was quite a space between the drift and the garage. I eased my way into the space, and began digging about half way along the length of the garage. As I worked, I could hear the music from Harry's stereo. It played softly and quietly so that meant Harry was probably not working yet. He was probably lying in his rumpled bed staring at the ceiling. He did that a lot. He always said that was his hardest work, but I figured he was joking.

I dug and dug and dug. The entrance was very narrow and low, forming a tunnel into the deepest part of the drift. The snow had to be pulled out, arm load by arm load, while lying on my belly. After more than an hour I had hollowed out enough of a living area, beyond the tunnel, to sit up in. Now the snow removal was slightly easier. Now I could push it out. I worked away for several more minutes, and was just beginning to feel satisfied with this initial effort, and hopeful for the end result when I heard Jennifer's voice in the distance.

"Pip! Pip! Where are you?"

I quickly squiggled over beside the tunnel where Jennifer would not be able to see me even if she did discover the entrance.

"Pip!" she screeched again a few minutes later. I sat perfectly still and held my breath. She was very close. "Pip, are you in there?" I sighed as Jennifer pulled herself inside my hideout and sat down beside me. "Kinda crowded," she said.

"It wasn't," I replied.

"What're you doing in here, anyway?" she asked.

"Hiding from you."

"Oh. Well, I found you. You left tracks."

"What d'ya want?" I whined.

"We gotta talk."

I sighed. That meant work, trouble, or both and always for me.

"Tomorrow, Pip, is the first of March and we still haven't found anyone for Mom."

I groaned and began digging away at the snow. My hideout was definitely too small.

"Hey!" cried Jennifer. You're getting snow all over *me*!"

"Then leave. I have work to do."

"But Pip! We have to save the house!"

I sank back against the wall. There was no use trying to fight her.

"The way I see it, Dr. Wiggins should be taken off the list of candidates. What do you think?"

"*Jennifer!* Mom still cries every time she goes into the dining room. I don't think we'll ever eat there again or use all that shiny stuff or anything. Maybe she'll never cook fried chicken again! And she keeps saying we've gotta get a new dentist!"

"So you agree or what?"

I nodded and pushed some more snow on Jennifer.

"Okay. Dr. Wiggins is now officially off the list. Now, who's next?"

I groaned and went back to my digging.

"I still think it should be a doctor," Jennifer said.

"And I still think it should be a baseball player."

"Oh, Pip! We have to move quickly. There isn't time to find one and then somehow get Mom together with him. I don't know how they'd ever meet. They're always traveling and we don't live anywhere near a team."

I kept digging. I was not about to tell her my plans. But she was right about one thing. I had to move fast, or Jennifer would get her pick.

"Now to get back to reality," Jennifer said. "I've found a Dr. O'Connell. He's never been married and he's just a year older than Mom and he's an Orthopedic Surgeon which means he makes scads of money."

I turned and stared at her. "How'd you find out all this stuff?"

"I phoned a bunch of doctors and told their secretaries I was doing a survey for a school project. They were very helpful."

"*Really?*"

"Yah. It was easy. Hardly anyone hung up on me and no one did a second time."

"Gee! I couldn't do something like that!" Jennifer's one-track mind could do some amazing things sometimes.

"So. You got anything wrong with you?" she asked.

"What do you mean?"

"Well, we have to come up with something. A bad leg or arm, maybe. *Something.*"

"Why?"

"So Mom has to take you to see this Dr. O'Connell."

"Oh, no!" I cried. "I went to the dentist. It's your turn!"

"I found him, didn't I? Did you phone fifty doctors and ask a dozen questions each? It's taken me days to do it!"

"But I…I…"

"And hours and hours to analyze the results!"

"But Jen…I…"

"*And you're the actor in the family.*"

"I am?"

"Oh, Pip, you're the greatest! You did the tooth part perfectly. Everybody believed you. *I could never do that!*"

"You couldn't?" She had me, and she knew it.

"Never. And now that you've done it once, it'll be a snap! Just change the menu to roast beef this time. It's Dr. O'Connell's favourite meal."

"You asked that, too?"

"Yup. Gotta think of everything. Now. What's going to be wrong with you?"

"I dunno."

"How about a bad leg? You just have to complain a lot to Mom and she'll take you to our doctor and she'll send you to the specialist. And I'll make certain she insists on Dr. O'Connell. Simple. Then you ask him over for supper. Make that dinner. It sounds more refined. Come on!"

"*Now?*"

"Now!"

"Jennifer, I'm building my secret hideout!"

"But I found it, so it's not secret anymore. So, there's no point. And anyway, you shouldn't be doing this. It's very, very dangerous. Don't you know anything? Come on!"

So we crawled out and I trudged after Jennifer but she stopped dead at the corner of the garage.

"There's Mom. Limp!" she ordered. It was not easy limping in two feet of snow. "See, Mom?" Jennifer called. "Pip's limping again!"

Mom stopped shoveling. "What? Limping? *Again*? What's wrong, Honey?"

"My leg hurts," I said, looking down at the snow to avoid her eyes. "I don't like lying to Mom," I whispered.

"Sssssssh! It's for her own good," Jennifer whispered. "Someday she'll thank you for it."

"You mean we gotta tell her about this someday?"

"Sssssssh! She's coming over."

"Maybe we should go inside and take a look." Mom took me into the house, and helped me off with my snowsuit, as if I had a broken leg. She got me onto the sofa and began to poke and prod. "Where does it hurt, Pip?"

"I dunno."

"The whole leg," supplied Jennifer.

"Well, maybe you're just cold," suggested Mom. "You've been outside a long time."

"It wasn't cold last week, Mom," said Jennifer.

"*Last week*? How long has this been going on?"

"Oh, weeks and weeks," said Jennifer.

"Weeks and weeks!" cried Mom. "Why hasn't someone *told* me?"

Jennifer shrugged. "Thought I did. Sorry."

I could hardly believe what I was hearing. Jennifer was lying like crazy and even I couldn't tell. "Wow!" I breathed.

"Did that hurt, Pip? Right there?" asked Mom.

"I guess so."

"Well, that's where my hand was when you said 'ow'."

"But I said…Yah, I guess," I murmured as Jennifer shot me a warning glance.

"Well, don't you worry, Pip," Mom said. "We're going to get this checked out right away."

But the check-up did little good. The doctor passed it off as growing pains and sent us home. Jennifer nagged me constantly and I ended up limping through the entire month of March.

"I think you should *insist* on seeing a specialist, Mom," Jennifer declared as Mom limped me back to the doctor. "A real *bone* specialist. I heard Dr. O'Connell is the best. My friend thinks he's wonderful and…"

"So you said, Jennifer," Mom cut in.

"I mean it, Mom. You have to *insist* on Dr. O'Connell."

"All right, all right."

And Mom did insist and we got an appointment for the end of April. But Jennifer still worried.

"I don't know if that leaves us enough time, Pip," she said as we sat on the back porch in the early spring sunshine and watched Harry walk in circles around our back yard. "I wish he'd quit talking to himself. I can't think."

"He's come up against the wall, Jennifer," I said.

"That's marathon running."

"It happens to writers, too. He's just working it out."

"Well, I wish he'd do it quietly. The talking's enough to drive you into the deeps, but that *howling*—"

"It's just the way he works," I said, adoringly.

"Anyway, Pip, the thing is, it's April already and the daffodils are blooming and it'll soon be fall and we'll be moving."

My heart sank. It had been such a nice day. Then I remembered my letter. I had changed my mind a dozen times on which athlete I wanted for a dad. It had been a much more difficult task than I'd ever thought it could be. It was even more difficult to compose the letter. But I had done it at last and over the past few days I had painstakingly written the letter out seven times, signed Mom's name, and mailed it to seven prospective fathers. I hadn't been able to decide on one in particular and I would have written to more, but I got tired of writing. But now that it was done all I needed to do was wait. And humour Jennifer. But just until Mom chose one of my guys. Boy, Jennifer's gonna be mad! I could hardly wait!

"If I could just remember which month we moved here," Jennifer said, bringing me back from my baseball dreams with a jerk. "I know we were here at Christmas. I remember the picture of us in front of the tree and it was here. But…that's it!" she squealed, leaping to her feet. "The photo album!"

As Jennifer disappeared into the house Harry let out a howl of agony that made my skin itch. Then he went back to his circular pacing, his head low, his hands clasped behind his back. Occasionally he'd shake his head back and forth and cover his eyes with his hands. And he muttered constantly. Something about Boogieland.

I heard a door open and looked over to see Mrs. Agatha Spencer come out on her back porch and stare at the mournful Harry. Harry suddenly let out a long and loud bloodcurdling howl of defeat, flopped onto his back on the grass and stared dejectedly up at the sky. Mrs. Agatha Spencer stomped over to her porch railing.

"Hey! You there!" she yelled at Harry. "What's all that ruckus about? You're upsetting my Spikey and if it keeps up it's going to wilt my daffodils!"

Harry seemed to hear nothing, but continued to stare at the sky and mumble about purple trees and orange seas.

"Hey! You there! I'm talking to you! *Are you deaf?*"

Harry suddenly grasped his hair by his hands, leapt up and let out a squeal of delight. "They fly!" he cried, leaping into the air. "The green horses fly!" Then he let out a perfectly wondrous howl and headed for his apartment. I clapped my hands, I was so happy his pain had ended.

But Mrs. Agatha Spencer continued to yell at him as he raced up his staircase. "If you don't stop that caterwauling I'm going to report you."

Harry gave her a confused look and disappeared inside his apartment. I knew he had no idea what she was talking about. But I did. I leapt to my feet and yelled back at her. "You leave Harry alone! He lives here and he can do anything he wants to."

"Not if it disturbs me, he can't," retorted Mrs. Agatha Spencer. "And if you don't show respect to your elders I'll report you, too."

Jennifer returned and plunked back down on the steps. She had a stack of photo albums and began paging through one.

"Doesn't your mother teach you any manners?" called Mrs. Agatha Spencer.

"Look, Pip," said Jennifer. "Here's one of me when I was a baby."

"You leave my mother alone!" I shrieked.

"Aren't I beautiful!" Jennifer cooed. "Oh, look at this one!"

"You keep it up, young fella," screeched Mrs. Agatha Spencer. "You just keep it up and I'll report you. See if I don't! Your mother ought to be ashamed!"

"You leave my mother alone, you old witch!" I screamed.

Jennifer discarded one album and picked up another. "Oh, look, Pip. Here's you as a baby. You were actually cute, then."

Suddenly Harry's stereo burst forth and the entire neighborhood was engulfed in the genius of Beethoven. I smiled. Harry was back at work.

"I'm warning you!" screamed Mrs. Agatha Spencer above the music. "I'll report the whole bunch of you, including that nut factory up there."

"He's not a nut factory!" I screamed.

Shaking her fist, Mrs. Agatha Spencer turned on her heel and with a slam of the door, disappeared from view.

"Harry is a first rate nut, you know," declared Jennifer.

"*He is not*!" I screamed.

"Oh, look!" said Jennifer. "Here's one of me holding you. And here you are with your birthday cake." I looked. Was that really me? "It was taken in the apartment. And look here!" I looked and saw a little witch complete with broom and hat. "That's me, and it was taken in the apartment, too." She flipped over the page. "And here we are in front of the Christmas tree and it's taken here in this house." I nodded. "So we moved here between Halloween and Christmas. And it's April now…so that leaves…at least seven months, maybe even eight. That should be long enough. What do you think?"

I shrugged and walked towards the garage. Halloween and Christmas. The regular baseball season was over a good month before Halloween, wasn't it? That must be tons of time to fall in love and get married before Christmas. Or, if it was a hockey player, they could fall in love this summer and get married before the regular season even started.

"Here comes Mom!" Jennifer called. And with that call I automatically began to limp up the stairs to Harry's apartment.

Inside, I could hear the rustling of papers and the soft murmur of Harry talking to his characters. I got out the peanut butter and bread, looked in the fridge and found the jam. I made several sandwiches and placed them on two plates. Then I found the pickles and mustard and added them to Harry's pile.

Wading through piles of crumpled paper, I walked across Harry's front room and quietly set Harry's plate of sandwiches beside him. Then I curled up in the big chair with Fluffy and fed bits of sandwich to each of us while I watched Harry work.

Pink skies and purple trees and bright red grass appeared as Harry's brush flew back and forth across his paper. Occasionally he reached out and took one of the sandwiches and ate a bite, unknowingly. His hands, working swiftly and smoothly now created horse-like creatures. Green horses. Beautiful green horses flying majestically through the pink skies. Then, as if by magic, a little boy appeared. A little boy with blond hair and a few freckles on his nose. It could have been me. Was it? Was Harry making a book with me in it? I thought of myself flying through the air, high above the tree tops, riding a majestic horse, it's wings beating the air, as we rose ever higher.

Harry, satisfied with his painting, went to his desk. I moved the remaining sandwiches over beside Harry. And while Harry's right hand, with pen gripped tightly, dashed excitedly back and forth across the page, his left hand picked up a sandwich.

I went back to the big chair and to Fluffy. I smiled contentedly as I stroked the big cat. It felt good to look after someone. Real good.

Chapter Nine

WHEN JENNIFER WASN'T ALLOWED TO GO

"**Y**ou look just fine, Pip," Mom said, giving me a hug. "Almost time to go." Suddenly Jennifer crashed through the door. "Jennifer! I thought you left for school."

"I did. But I just thought of something."

"Well hurry up! You're going to be late!"

"But Mom, why can't I go with Pip?"

"Because you have to go to school, Jennifer. We've been through this before."

"But you're supposed to be at work."

"Jennifer, listen a moment, please," Mom said as she put her arm around Jennifer. "I know you're used to mothering Pip when I'm not here and I appreciate that. He couldn't ask for a better big sister." My eyes grew big. Was Mom *listening* to herself? "But at times like this he needs his real mother and his real mother needs him. Okay?"

"But I could go, too! He might need me!"

"Yes, he might, Dear, but he'll just have to rely on me this time. Just this once. Now hurry. You're really going to be late."

"Okay, okay. But I gotta tell Pip something."

"Make it fast. I'll go get our jackets and Pip's x-rays."

"What now?" I asked.

"Just wanted to remind you that it's *roast beef* he likes."

"I *remember*." She'd only told me three zillion times.

"Okay. Good luck. It's all up to you now. But I was thinking, Pip. Don't bother asking him over if he's ugly."

"What?"

"But make sure he's real ugly. Don't just cop out. I'm going to check on him if you don't ask and if I don't think he's real ugly, I'll reach in your mouth and pull your tongue right out of your head."

"*What?*"

"If he's just not very good looking, go for it, okay?"

"What's ugly got to do with it? Mom says it's what's on the inside that counts."

"Yah, yah. Now listen up. You gotta think things through, Pip. If he and Mom got married and he was real ugly, you know, the baby might look like him and then we'd have this real ugly baby around all the time."

"*Baby?*" I hadn't thought of a baby. A baby brother might be nice. Then I'd have someone to play catch with whenever I wanted.

"*Think* about it, Pip. Everywhere we'd go there'd be people shrieking, 'Look at that ugly baby!' You wouldn't like that, would you?"

"I guess not."

"Well, Mom wouldn't like it either and it'd be all your fault because you didn't think about people pointing at her in her stroller."

"Her?"

"Yah. Your baby sister."

Thoughts of playing catch vanished with a thud. "How do you know it's a sister?"

"Girls just know these things."

"Oh." I wished boys did.

"Jennifer!" yelled Mom.

"Coming!" Jennifer yelled back. "So just remember the roast beef, Pip, and the ugly part, and you'll be fine."

"Okay."

"Good luck. Our baby sister's future depends on you. Gotta go."

I felt my shoulders getting heavy.

"Wasn't that sweet of your sister?" asked Mom, as she came into the living room. "She ran all the way back from school to wish you well. Not many brothers or sisters would be so sweet."

I nodded glumly and followed Mom out the back door. *Two sisters*! Maybe Harry would let me move in with him. Harry probably wouldn't even notice if I did. I could sleep in the big chair with Fluffy.

"All ready?" asked Harry as he came down the apartment stairs.

"Yes, thank you, Harry," answered Mom.

All ready? Thank you? Can't be!

"This is so thoughtful of you, Harry. It'll save us a dreadfully long bus ride."

Can be! And was! Wow! We were going in Harry's car.

I climbed onto the tiny back seat, Mom and the x-rays took the front seat next to Harry and Fluffy leapt onto Harry's shoulder and growled at Mom.

"I…I didn't know Fluffy was going, too," Mom said. Her voice sounded strangely small.

"Fluffy goes where I…uh…go," said Harry as he gave Fluffy a scratch behind the ears. "Unless he…uh…doesn't want to. Everyone…uh…buckled up?"

Everyone but Fluffy was buckled up. Harry put the car in gear, stepped on the gas and roared backward, out of our driveway, across the street, and up Jeff's driveway. Harry slammed on the brakes and everyone jerked forward.

"Wonderful things…uh…seat belts, don't you…uh…think?" asked Harry as we roared out onto the street. "So…uh…how are you, Pip?" Harry asked, shifting gears and turning around in his seat at the same time. Mom screamed! Harry hit the brakes! Mrs. Agatha Spencer wet her pants! Then she left the crosswalk, picked up a stone and hurled it at the car. "She seems a bit…uh…testy today," Harry said as he stepped on the gas throwing us all back into our seats.

"We *could* take the bus from here," gasped Mom. "It'd be no trouble."

"Nonsense!" cried Harry, turning around in his seat again. "You don't want to take the…uh…bus do you, Pip?"

"Gosh, no!" I cried.

"Pip!" groaned Mom. Then she screamed again.

"Oooooops," said Harry as a car, honking furiously, roared off. "Was that a stop sign?"

"Well, that one got away, anyway," gasped Mom. "Do you know where we're going?"

"Uh…no. Can't say that I…uh…do." Harry pulled out around a car and narrowly missed an oncoming truck.

"Well, then, just let us out somewhere along here. It's not far. The walk will do us good."

"Mom!" I screeched. "It's miles yet!"

"*Pip!*"

"Why not just tell me where…uh…you're going?" suggested Harry.

"The Medical Centre on Collins Boulevard," I said.

"*PIP!*" exclaimed Mom. What was wrong with her, anyway?

"*Collins Boulevard?*" cried Harry. "I'm in the…uh…wrong lane!" He wheeled over to the left, sending everyone flopping to the right. Horns honked. Tires screeched. And Fluffy growled as he landed on the seat beside Mom. As we entered the intersection, Harry wheeled hard to the left again. "Oooops," he said. "The light turns to…

uh...red real quick, doesn't it?" Cars swerved out of the way. Tires squealed. And I heard, from somewhere behind us, the scrunch of metal. Fluffy was spitting and growling at Mom who was huddled in the corner, with the x-ray package over her face. "There, now," said Harry. "Just straight ahead from...uh...here."

Fluffy leapt back on Harry's shoulders and, still growling, waved a warning paw at Mom, who slowly pulled her hands down from her face. She looked very pale.

"Are you sick, Mom?" I asked.

"Yes," squeaked Mom.

"Well," said Harry. "Good thing we're going to a...uh...medical centre."

Opposite the building, Harry swerved across the path of oncoming traffic and roared into the parking lot.

"Smelled that driver's breath," gasped Mom.

"Pardon?" asked Harry. "Ah! Lucky us! A parking place right...uh...here."

"Lucky us," groaned Mom.

"If you're sick, Mom, we could just go home," I suggested, hopefully.

"Oh, I'm sure I'll be just dandy in a minute," Mom mumbled. "Just as soon as someone peels me out of this seat."

"Well, let's...uh...go." said Harry with a big smile. "You protect the...uh...car, Fluffy, while we're gone."

Fluffy growled and spit as Mom unbuckled her seat belt. She reached over and patted the startled cat on the head. "You don't scare me, anymore, cat," she said. "I'm now scare proof! Nothing can faze me now!"

I took a closer look at her. There was definitely *something* wrong with her.

"You don't have to wait, Harry," she said. "We can catch a bus home."

"No, no…uh…no!" exclaimed Harry, hoisting me up over his shoulder. "I have to…uh…stick by my buddy."

"If you insist," said Mom, "but may I see your car keys for a minute?" Harry handed Mom his keys. "I'm driving home."

"Ah, Mom!" I whined as I watched her march across the parking lot.

"She…uh…seems a tad upset about something," commented Harry as we watched her disappear through the revolving doors. She was waiting for us just inside the doors and we followed her, silently, into the elevators and then down the hall to Dr. O'Connell's waiting room where Harry deposited me on a chair. Four comic books later the lady at the desk called my name.

"Good…uh…luck, Pip! I'll wait for you by the elevators," Harry said, and left.

Mom put her arm around my shoulders and walked me into the examining room. She introduced us and handed Dr. O'Connell the x-rays.

"Nice to meet you," the doctor said. Then he lowered his eyes to the floor and slowly raised them until he was looking at Mom's face again. It was like he had measured us with his eyes. Mom's face turned dark pink. "*Very* nice to meet you," he said and I didn't like the way he said it. It made me feel squirmy inside. He took the x-rays out of the envelope and placed them on a shelf thingy and turned a light on behind them. He kept saying, "Uh-huh, uh-huh," as he looked.

I watched him very carefully. Was he ugly? I didn't think so.

"Well, Philip," the doctor said as he flicked off the light. How about taking those pants off and letting me see how you walk."

I took off my sneakers, then pulled my jeans off inside out. While Mom turned the pants right side out and undid the knots in my sneakers, I walked back and forth for Dr. O'Connell.

"What's your daddy do?" the doctor asked.

"Huh?"

"We're divorced," Mom said, struggling with a knot. "We never see him."

"I see," Dr. O'Connell said. He was smiling *that* smile. The same smile I had seen Dr. Wiggins smile! "You have very nice legs, Philip. You must take after your mother."

I glanced at Mom. Her eyes were big and her mouth had dropped about three inches.

"Now, son," the doctor said, "up on the table."

Son! He was already calling me *son*! I looked at Mom but she was still standing there with her mouth open and one still-knotted shoe in her hand. The doctor began pushing my legs back and forth. "Bet your mother has lots of boy friends, eh Philip?" I shook my head. "No? A pretty lady like her? Maybe it's girl friends, is it?"

"What?" I asked.

"*Dr. O'Connell!*" gasped Mom, coming towards us, the knotted shoe still in her hand.

The doctor laughed. "Just asking, just asking. No offense. Never been married myself."

Mom gave herself a little shake, took a deep breath and went back to my shoelace.

"I think I see the problem," the doctor said. Not serious enough for surgery but—"

"*Surgery!*" shrieked Mom.

"Oh, don't worry, you brought him in time. A brace for a few months should do the trick."

"*A brace!*" I gasped.

The doctor wrote something on a piece of yellow paper and handed it to Mom. "Just take this downstairs to the workshop and get him suited up. Then bring him back to see me in three months."

Mom stared at the paper. "A brace?" she whispered.

"He won't have to wear it all the time. Just at night and whenever he's relaxing in front of the television and such. It won't interfere with his life."

"Oh," breathed Mom, putting the paper in her purse. "But our doctor said it was just growing pains."

"Well, your doctor isn't a specialist, now is he?" Dr. O'Connell said. Mom's lips seemed to disappear. "Now, young man, you get dressed and I'll show your mother these x-rays."

I pulled on my pants. But the snap wouldn't snap. I put on my one shoe and wondered if Mom had unknotted the one she was holding. I laced up the shoe and then tried my pants again. It just wouldn't snap. I looked at Mom and wondered if I should ask for help. She was standing next to the doctor and looking at my x-rays on the wall.

"See the difference between these two legs?" the doctor was saying as his left hand pointed and his right arm went around Mom's shoulders. I wondered if now was a good time to mention the roast beef. I struggled with the snap again. I'd *told* Jennifer I shouldn't wear these pants. It was always hard to get the snap done up, and the zipper wouldn't stay up unless the snap was snapped.

"Mom?" I asked, and hobbled over towards her in my one shoe and holding my pants up.

The doctor was looking at Mom in a very odd way. I had seen that look before. But where? *On Spike*! That was it. Just before he pounced!

"How about dinner?" asked Dr. O'Connell as his hand slipped down to Mom's bottom.

"*Pardon?*" asked Mom.

"We're both unattached, both lonely," he said, as he gave her bottom a pat.

Mom's hand, with my shoe still in it, came up and whacked Dr. O'Connell.

"*Susan!*"

"Don't Susan me!" cried Mom. "*How dare you!*"

"I'm sorry. I just thought—"

"Well, you thought wrong! Come on, Pip!" She grabbed my hand and pulled me towards the door. The doctor jumped in front of us and barred the way.

"It's all a misunderstanding, Susan," he gasped. "I'm so sorry. Just dinner. That's all."

"No misunderstanding, Doctor. Just get out of my way!" cried Mom.

It was now or never. "Do you like roast beef?" I asked.

"*PIP!*" screeched Mom. "Now, *Doctor*, get out of my way or do you want the shoe again?"

"Look, let's talk this over, Susan," Dr. O'Connell pleaded.

"You didn't like my son's shoe?" asked Mom. "*Then how about mine?*"

I gasped as Mom stabbed his shoe with her spike heel and when he yelped and grabbed for his foot Mom pushed him over.

"Believe, me, doctor, this was not the morning to try anything with me," Mom said, her words spitting angry for some reason. "Even *you* cannot faze me."

"Are you all right, doctor?" the receptionist called.

"He's fine!" Mom called back. "Just fine!"

"I'll call, okay? We'll talk," the doctor said through clenched teeth.

Right now, lying on the floor holding his foot like that, the doctor did look kind of ugly. I'd just have to hope Jennifer agreed. I rather liked having a tongue.

Mom yanked the door open and yanked me through it. Everyone in the waiting room stared as Mom marched through, with me scrambling along behind her, still holding my pants up and wearing only one shoe. It was a relief to get out into the hall and see Harry.

"Susan!" cried Harry, as he leapt up from the bench`. "Pip! How…uh…are you, Buddy? What'd the doc say?"

"My pants!" I shrieked as Harry hoisted me up over his shoulders, and my pants fell down around my ankles.

But Harry didn't notice. "What'd he...uh...say?"

Mom didn't notice either. She sat on the bench with her head in her hands.

"Harry, my pants!"

"What's...uh...wrong, Susan?" Harry asked, his voice soft and low. "What'd the...uh...doctor say?"

"That I had nice legs," mumbled Mom, from behind her hands.

"What?" gasped Harry.

"And I guess he liked my bottom, too," she groaned.

"*What?*" cried Harry, dropping me to the floor. I quickly yanked up my pants.

"Where is that...uh—"

"No!" cried Mom, raising her head from her lap. "Don't, Harry!"

"*What do you mean...uh...DON'T?*" cried Harry. "I'll beat his ugly...uh...face in until—"

Whew, I thought, Harry thinks he's ugly, too.

"Please, Harry!" begged Mom. "No heroics. I need you to *help* me. I need you to bring Pip back in three months for a check-up. I just can't."

"Of...uh...course, Susan. Whatever you...uh...say." Harry sat down beside Mom and put his arm around her. Mom put her head on his shoulder and began to cry.

"Mom, how come you don't hit Harry when he puts his arm around you?" I asked.

"You *hit* him?" asked Harry, taking another look at Mom.

"Yah! It was neat! She hit him with my shoe."

"You're...uh...kidding!" cried Harry, grinning.

Mom shook her head and began to giggle. "You should have seen his face!"

"Can I have my shoe back now?" I asked.

Mom handed me my shoe. "And even after I stomped on his foot—"

"*You stomped on his...uh...foot?*" cried Harry.

"Yah! And then she gave him a big push and he fell on the floor," I said. I was suddenly very proud of my Mom.

Mom and Harry were laughing, now, but I was sitting on the floor still struggling to untie the knot in my sneaker.

"Even then," laughed Mom, "he said he'd call me."

"Well," laughed Harry, "we'd better go...uh...right over to the phone company and...uh...get you an unlisted number."

"But first we have to get Pip fitted for a brace," Mom declared, as she got shakily to her feet.

"*A brace!*" cried Harry.

"It's all right, Harry," Mom said. "He's going to be just fine."

"My...uh...poor little guy!" crooned Harry, coming over and picking me up.

"No!" I screeched as my pants fell down again.

But Harry was already buzzing for the elevator. "Do you...uh... think I can afford to take us out for...uh...supper tonight?"

"Yes, Harry, it's fine."

"Then let's get Jennifer and go to someplace...uh...real nice. We...uh...need to celebrate your heroism!'"

Harry smiled at Mom as we got on the elevator. Mom smiled at Harry. Then she saw me. "Pip! For goodness sakes, do up your pants."

Chapter Ten

WHEN JENNIFER NEEDED MONEY

"I'm really sorry, Pip," Jennifer said as she helped me on with my brace. "You fake a toothache and have to get a filling and—"

"Two."

"Two. And you fake a bad leg and end up with a brace. And all for nothing! What are we going to do?"

"Does this mean we're going to lose the house, Jen?" I asked.

"I guess."

The brace now on, she helped me get comfortable on the couch. "But I can't sleep if I'm not in my own bed."

"You will, eventually."

"On a floor somewhere?"

"I guess," sighed Jennifer. We could pretend we're camping. I just hope we can afford a place with a kitchen."

"A *kitchen!*" I cried. "You mean some places don't have kitchens?"

"That's what I've heard." She slumped back against the cushions.

"But, Jen!"

"Some places don't even have bathrooms."

"*Jen!*"

"You have to share one down the hall with a bunch of other people," she sighed.

"*JEN!*"

"Unless..." She sighed again.

"Unless what?"

"Unless we take in boarders. Let's see. I could have your room--"

"My room! What's wrong with yours?"

"It's bigger. You and Mom will have to share it."

"What's wrong with *hers*?"

"It's the biggest. We'll have to rent it out. It's big enough for two people to share. And then the guest room can be rented and the den. That's four. I figure that'll give us more than enough. Should be enough left over for a really super Barbie House. And a Barbie Pool and Patio Set. Lots of—"

"*Jennifer! My room!*" I wailed.

"You want your bed, don't you? and a bathroom and a kitchen? You're so greedy, Pip."

"But you're getting a bunch of Barbie stuff. Why can't I have a bunch of Lego?"

"That's because I'm a girl. Honestly, Pip, don't you know *anything*?"

I didn't say anymore. My leg ached. Really. And now I felt stupid, again. Then I remembered the letters I'd written to the athletes and that made me feel better. I wondered if I should tell Jennifer about them. No. She'd probably just get mad at me.

Suddenly the back doorbell rang and Wendy rushed in. "Where's your Mom?"

"Upstairs. In the tub," Jennifer replied.

Wendy ran up the stairs, two at a time.

"Won't we be kind of crowded, Jen?" I asked.

"I guess, but we'll still have a kitchen. I *think* that's more important."

Now I felt stupid again. I heard Mom and Wendy shriek with laughter, and a few moments later, Wendy ran down the stairs, and out the door.

"And we'd have to cook and do all those dishes for all those people," I groaned.

"We'll be able to afford a dishwasher."

"Oh." Maybe the idea wasn't totally awful.

"Sssssssh!" whispered Jennifer, as Mom came down the stairs with a towel wrapped around her head.

"What were you and Wendy laughing about, Mom?" I asked.

"It's probably just for ladies, Pip," Jennifer said.

"Oh that," laughed Mom. "That crazy Wendy has gone and signed up with a computer dating service." Toweling her hair, she ambled off into the kitchen.

Jennifer sat up. "Computer dating service?" she whispered. "But that's it!" she shrieked. She jumped off the couch, grabbed me, and hurried into the kitchen.

"Not so fast!" I cried, trying to keep up with my leg hobbled in a brace.

"Just how does a computer dating service work, exactly?" asked Jennifer as we entered the kitchen. Mom was just sitting down with her coffee. Jennifer poured herself a glass of milk then pulled up a chair beside Mom. She grabbed me and pulled me into the chair next to her.

"Well, it's kind of silly, really," Mom said. "I mean, it's not very romantic."

"But how does it work?"

"You fill in a questionnaire telling what you're like and what you enjoy doing and what you'd like in a partner. And you supply some photos of yourself. Then the computer tries to match you up with someone who fits—"

"Someone like you asked for?"

"And shares similar interests."

"What's silly about that? Sounds perfectly logical to me."

"Well, yes, but it's just that it's not very romantic."

"What's romantic?" I asked.

"Oh, I don't know, Pip. I guess it's meeting someone out of pure chance and then falling madly in love."

"Like that isn't silly," said Jennifer. "Realistically, what are the odds of that happening with a really great guy, Mom? Especially with one who has money."

"Not very good, I guess, but that's how I met your father.... Never mind. Bad example."

"See what I mean? Kind of chancy, no matter how you look at it. So let's get you signed up."

"*Me?*"

"Why not?" I asked. Maybe my bedroom could be saved after all.

"I don't want to."

"Why not? I bet the computer would get you a ball player! Or a hockey player!"

"Oh, Pip," groaned Jennifer.

"I'm simply not looking for a man."

"*You're not?*" And I'd written all those letters! And I had 2 fillings and now a brace!

"No, I'm not. I'm very happy with my life the way it is."

"*You are?*" I asked. Would she be angry when one of the athletes asked her to marry him? What if all seven did?

"Yes, Pip, I am. No offence, but a man is not essential to a woman's happiness. Of course, my job is rather boring, but then, it isn't exhausting either. It pays well, as jobs go, but I suppose I'll always have problems making ends meet." Mom sighed. "I would like to have more time for you two. And a reliable car to take us places…and oh, my goodness, *I just don't know what we'll do about university!*"

"Mom?"

"Yes, Pip?"

"Are you going to cry?"

"No. No, I'm not. We'll manage. Don't you worry about it."

"Can I go over to Wendy's?" asked Jennifer.

"She's got a date."

"Just for a second, Mom, please."

"I suppose."

Jennifer flew out the door and I walked, stiff-legged, into the living room. I flopped back onto the couch and turned on the television.

"Is it awful having that brace on, Hon?" Mom asked as she entered the room.

"Yah. Kinda."

"Well, try to keep it in perspective."

"Pers…what?"

"Perspective. Don't give it any more importance than it deserves. Try to remember that although the brace is a big nuisance now, it's better than having pain for the rest of your life."

I felt my cheeks burn. "Yah, Mom. Sure."

Mom kissed me on the forehead and went to the laundry room. A moment later Jennifer ran in, puffing. "Wendy's going to help!" she exclaimed in an excited whisper.

I sighed and turned off the TV. I knew she wouldn't let me watch it now. "Help what?" I asked.

"She's going to pick up the forms and help me fill them in."

"What forms?"

"Computer Dating! Where do you live, anyway?"

"But, Jen, Mom said she didn't want to join," I protested.

"Didn't you hear her worrying about our university? Don't you want to help your own mother?"

"Jen, she said she didn't want to join."

"What Mom doesn't know, won't hurt her!"

"*Jennifer!*"

"You want your bedroom back, don't you?"

"Yah, but—"

"There's a catch, though."

"What?"

"It costs a lot of money to join."

"A lot of money!" I shrieked.

"Did you call, Pip?" Mom called from the laundry room.

"No, Mom," I yelled back.

"Boy, Pip! Try and think, would you?"

"But, Jen, where are we going to get money?"

"Remember the garage sale at Brenda's?"

"*We're not selling my bed!*"

"Pip, are you okay?" Mom called.

"He's fine, Mom," Jennifer called. "I'm with him now."

"And that makes me fine?"

"Would you keep your voice down, please! Now listen. We'll just sell everything we don't need anymore."

"Like what?"

"Oh, your Lego and—"

"*Not my Lego!*"

"Sssssssh! Jeepers, Pip. Keep a lid on it."

I gritted my teeth. "You're *not* selling my Lego!"

"Think of bathrooms, Pip, and kitchens, and blankets on the floor, and Mom crying."

"You're *not* selling my Lego!"

"Okay, okay. Have it your way. Just your old games and stuff."

"What about your old games and stuff."

"Yah, yah. And Wendy says some people sell baking at these things, and lemonade."

"So?"

"So I'll bake some cookies and you make some lemonade."

So Jennifer began filling the freezer with her cookies and I began keeping a watchful eye on Jennifer. "Where'd you put my race track, Jennifer?"

"In the garage."

"You can't sell my race track! And where's my crane?"

"Pip you never play with it."

"I do, too. And how about my micro machines?"

"Pip! Think! The bathroom? The blanket on the floor?"

"*NO!*"

"Suit yourself. We'll see who's crying this Christmas."

"Ah, Jen!"

Every time I went into my room, I had to check to see what was missing. There was always something.

"Wendy says we can let others come to sell stuff and charge them for coming, Mom. Okay?" asked Jennifer.

"Mmmmmm," said Mom, who was balancing her chequebook.

Jennifer persuaded a lot of our friends to come and sell things, too. She made notices for bulletin boards which read 'Giant Kids Sale'.

"There's giant kids coming?" I laughed. Jennifer scowled.

Harry drove Jennifer to two malls and five Laundromats where she tacked up her notices on every bulletin board she could find.

"How about you, Mom?" asked Jennifer. "Got anything you want to get rid of?"

"Probably."

"It'll only cost you five dollars."

Mom laughed. "I think you're on your way to Big Business, Jennifer. Tell you what. I'll gather up some things and you two can look after them and split whatever money you take in between you."

"See, Pip?" Jennifer said later. "She must want to join computer dating or she wouldn't be helping us raise the money."

"But, Jen, she doesn't know what the money's for!"

"Of course she does."

"She does? You told?"

"No. I just know that deep down inside she knows."

"How do you know *that*?"

"Girls simply know these things, that's all."

I sighed and went back to my room to see what else was missing. On the night before the sale, I did sleep on a blanket right in front of my door so Jennifer would trip over me if she tried to sneak in and steal more of my things.

On the day of the sale we had to get up very early. "Wendy says it doesn't matter what time you advertise, people start coming at eight," Jennifer informed us.

So at seven I began dragging things out to the front lawn. All the kids had blankets to put their things on and everyone had a box to put their money in.

"Eleven kids!" exclaimed Jennifer. "That's a lot of money already! Where's your money, Pip?"

"Jennifer!"

"Okay, okay. Let's go get the kitchen table to put Mom's stuff on."

"But everybody else has blankets," I argued.

"But we live here. We can have a table."

We hauled out the table and set it on the lawn next to the front walk and piled Mom's stuff on it. We piled our things on a blanket next to the table. Then we put the lemonade, paper cups, and cookies on our folding tables.

People came. People bought. Jennifer sold our things and I sold lemonade and cookies. Kids and their parents were everywhere buying things for quarters, ones and even five and ten dollar bills.

It was fun. It kept me busy keeping my two pitchers filled with lemonade. I took in a lot of money. All of the other kids were having fun, too. "Look how much money I've got, Pip!" they'd call or "I sold all my old puzzles!"

The kids who were buying stuff seemed happy, too. "Look at this neat game I bought for only a dollar, Mom," or "see my beautiful new doll!" And then, "Look at all this Lego I bought for only ten dollars."

"Who sold their Lego?" I yelled. Everyone stopped what they were doing and looked at me like I was crazy. "*My Lego!*" I cried and ran after the boy. "That's my Lego!" I yelled and grabbed the box and pulled. The boy pulled back.

"It's mine. I paid for it!" he yelled.

"But it's stolen property!" I screamed.

The boy's mother began screaming at us to stop. We didn't. The box began to rip.

Suddenly two hands clamped down on the box. "What's...uh...wrong, Pip?" asked Harry. We stopped pulling and let Harry take the box.

"Jennifer sold him my Lego," I cried, tears stinging the back of my eyes. "She stole it and sold it.

"How...uh...much, fella?" he asked.

"Ten bucks and I'm not selling."

"He bought it fair and square," said the boy's mother.

Harry dug in his pockets and pulled out a twenty dollar bill.

"No way!" said the boy.

My tears moved from the back of my eyes to the front. Harry dug some more. "All I have is a...uh...fifty," he said pulling the bill out.

"Sold!" cried the boy as he grabbed the bill and ran.

"Hey! Give Harry the twenty back!" I yelled.

"Let him...uh...go, Pip," said Harry. "Is it worth seventy dollars?"

"Way, way more than seventy," I said, wiping my tears on my sleeve.

"Then it's...uh...okay," said Harry, giving me a hug.

"Thanks, Harry. Jennifer stole it. I slept in front of my door last night and everything, but she still got it."

"Well, I'll have to have a little...uh...talk with Jennifer."

Harry talked to Jennifer and she said she was sorry and would never do it again.

"You owe Harry seventy dollars!" I exclaimed. Her face fell.

"How about taking it out in...uh...trade?" suggested Harry. He picked up a giant teddy bear.

"But that's mine," said Jennifer. Harry pointed to the Lego and Jennifer nodded. "His name is Bear." Harry smiled and put the bear under one arm, the Lego under the other. "Are you going to tell on me, Harry?" Harry shook his head. "Thanks, Harry."

"You can come visit Bear anytime," he said.

Harry carried the Lego up to my room for me, and then he took Bear home.

When I got back to the table, the table wasn't there and what was left of Mom's things was crowded onto our blanket.

"Where's the table, Jen?" I asked.

"Well, I sort of got carried away, kind of."

"*Jennifer!*"

"But he dangled a fifty dollar bill in front of me and begged. *Begged*, Pip! What could I say?"

"No. *You coulda said NO!*"

"It's too late now."

"*What are we going to do for a table?*" I cried. This couldn't be happening!

"We've got the dining room table, Pip. It's not like we're going to eat on the floor. Now go get another blanket."

I went and got another blanket. When I got back to our blanket most of the things were gone and so was our blanket. I turned and fled with the second blanket clutched firmly in my arms. It wasn't safe out there!

"She was way out of control, Mom," I said when I sat down at the dining room table with her and Harry that evening. "She just turned into a raving loony!"

"I shouldn't have left," moaned Mom. "But it was a Saturday Only Special and you needed new pants so badly! And I intended to rush right back but then Jean came along and we hadn't seen each other for so long! And I knew Harry was here if you needed help. Harry, I'm so sorry, I should have come home sooner."

"Mom!" called Jennifer from the kitchen. "Can I come in there? *Please!*"

"No, Jennifer," said Mom. "You most certainly cannot."

I could hear Jennifer plunking her plate down on the floor. "Fudgie!" she groaned.

Chapter Eleven

WHEN JENNIFER GOT CAUGHT

"Help me with this stuff, will you, Pip?" Jennifer asked.

I picked up a box and followed Jennifer down the stairs and out the door. "Where are you taking all this stuff?"

"Wendy's."

"Why?"

"She wants it."

"Why does she want all your books and Playmobile, Jen?" I asked between puffs.

"Collateral. She wanted my Barbie stuff, too, but I managed to talk her into letting me have *something*."

"What's collateral?"

"What you have to have to get a loan. She's keeping all this stuff until I pay her back. It's like a guarantee."

"A guarantee?" I asked, again not understanding.

"Yah," Jennifer said and set down her box while she unlatched the gate. "To have enough for the Dating Service."

"Oh."

"I would have had almost enough, too, if Mom hadn't made me give her the money for the table."

"And the blanket."

"Yah, the blanket, too." She kicked the gate angrily and stomped through.

"They were her things, Jen," I reminded her.

"I know, I know, but jeepers, Pip, she wouldn't have had that money if it wasn't for me!"

"But Jen—"

"And I had it right in my hand and she took it right out. Oh Pip! That's such an awful experience! You know?"

I didn't know. I suspected it was another thing that only girls knew. We carried the boxes into Wendy's and put them in the hall closet.

"I don't know why Pip shouldn't have to give some collateral, too," Jennifer whined.

"You just leave Pip out of this," said Wendy, giving me a big smile. "Now let's fill in the questionnaire."

I went back home. I had quit limping now, and no one asked about my leg. I figured in another week or so, I'd quit using the brace and if no one said anything I'd hide it in my closet and we could all forget about it.

Mom was just opening the mail, when I walked into the kitchen. "That's odd," she said. "Here's a letter for me from Florida. I don't know anyone in Florida."

I gasped. Could it be? "Open it!"

Mom opened it and as she read it, her eyebrows went up and up.

"What's it say?"

"Some crack pot has gotten hold of my address!" exclaimed Mom. "Basically, he says he's sorry he can't marry me but he doesn't even like women."

I fled to Harry's. When I opened his door, Fluffy scuttled out. Inside, I found Harry deeply engrossed in his book about the flying horses and the little boy who looked like me.

After making Harry some peanut butter, jam, mustard and pickle sandwiches I curled up in the big chair with Bear and looked out the window. Harry, working diligently at his desk did not seem to notice me, but the sandwiches slowly and steadily disappeared. I watched Fluffy hop onto Mrs. Agatha Spencer's fence and edge his way slowly and carefully along it. Spike was sleeping on Mrs. Agatha Spencer's back porch. It was a warm, sleepy sort of day and I had to blink to keep from drifting off as I watched Fluffy jump off the fence and amble over towards the porch. Spike woke up and stared at the approaching cat. I sat up, my eyes wide open, now, with fear. Fluffy sat down and had a bath.

"Fluffy!" I cried, and ran out the door and down the steps. As I rounded the corner of the garage, I saw Spike jump off the step. Fluffy leapt into the air, flipped around and landed on the run. He leapt over the fence and streaked towards our old Chestnut tree. Spike flew over the fence, hot on the heels of Fluffy. But Fluffy shot up the Chestnut tree and crouched on its lowest branch and growled and spit at Spike who was now leaping up and barking at Fluffy.

"Oh, Fluffy!" I cried taking a step towards the tree. "You're okay!" Suddenly Spike turned his head towards me, and I realized where I was and who I was with in the yard! With a terrified yelp I ran for our back door. I could feel Spike's hot smelly breath on my legs when I slammed the door behind me. Spike smashed into it and a moment later Mrs. Agatha Spencer was once again yelling at me from her porch. I leaned against the door and gasped for breath. My legs shook. It was a full five minutes before I felt able to walk upstairs to my room. And even then, flopped on my bed with a book, I could feel my legs trembling.

Before I had read two pages, Jennifer trotted in and plunked herself onto my bed beside me.

"Oh, Pip!" she exclaimed. "You missed all the fun! It was just like Christmas, only I was ordering a father instead of Barbie stuff."

I groaned. I should have stayed! "What did you order?"

"Someone with money who likes to have fun."

"But Mom doesn't like to have fun!" I said.

"Sure she does. I put that down, too."

"But she doesn't!"

"Pip, *everybody* likes to have fun. Mom just can't afford to have fun, that's all. She's friends with Wendy, isn't she, so she must be like her. I know she'd just love to go to dances and parties like Wendy does."

"But she *doesn't!*" I insisted. I sure didn't want babysitters all the time even if the babysitter was Jeff.

"Look, Pip, just leave it to me, okay? The forms are all filled out and Wendy is taking them to the Dating Service right now."

"But, Jen, I really don't think Mom wants to go to a bunch of parties and stuff."

"Of course she does. Wendy says so, too."

"How do you know?" I asked, but as soon as I blurted it out, I knew exactly what the answer would be.

"We girls know these things, that's all," Jennifer said.

Three days later, I began to wonder about girls knowing everything.

"It's for you, Mom," Jennifer called from the kitchen. Mom turned the vacuum off and went into the kitchen. "It's a man!" Jennifer whispered in my ear. I was building a Lego castle on the living room floor. "Come on!"

Reluctantly, I followed Jennifer out to the kitchen and arrived just in time to see Mom slam the receiver down.

"Of all the nerve!" she cried.

"What, Mom?" asked Jennifer. "What did he say?"

"He wanted to know if I was ready to *parrr-teee!*"

"Well, maybe he's really nice and wants to take you to a party. Did you give him a chance?"

Mom's mouth dropped and she stared at Jennifer for the longest time. "*Give him a chance?*" she shrieked. "Anybody who calls me *Babe* and wants to *parrr-teee* does not need a chance! Not from me, anyway!" She stalked out of the room and turned the vacuum back on. I scowled at Jennifer.

"The next one will be more polite," she assured me.

But the next one wanted to 'Get Down' and Mom hung up on him, too. Hard.

"Just what is going on?" cried Mom when she'd slammed the receiver down on the fifth caller in four days. "I've got an unlisted phone. Where are these weirdos getting my number?"

"I guess we leaned too heavily on the fun and not heavily enough on the money," was all Wendy could say about it.

The very next day Mom received her second letter. "What's it say, Mom?" I asked, holding my breath.

Mom shook her head. "I simply cannot understand why all this is happening to me. Phone calls! Letters! Where do people get my number? my address? and why now, all of a sudden?"

"But what does the letter say?" I repeated, though hope was dwindling fast.

Mom sighed. "He says he'd love to marry me, but his girlfriend won't let him. And, odd as it may seem, both letters were from professional baseball players. From Jays, actually." She shook her head and tossed the letter into the garbage. There went my bedroom!

Eleven days and a dozen or more phone calls after the questionnaire had been delivered to the Dating Service, the phone rang and I answered it. This time the caller said he was doing a survey and asked for the address. I gave it to him. Later, when Jennifer and I were doing the dishes and Mom was doing laundry, Harry and Fluffy came in. Harry was carrying a bundle of papers.

"My...uh...lights won't come on," Harry said.

"Mom!" Jennifer yelled. "Harry's lights don't work."

"Did you check the breaker?" Mom asked as she came in the kitchen.

"Breaker? Uh...no."

"I'll go check." When she came back in, she was holding a Disconnect Notice. "You didn't pay your bill, Harry."

"Uh...sorry."

"Told you he was a bum," whispered Jennifer. "It'll be the rent next."

Then we heard it. We all stopped what we were doing and looked out the window and watched as a big black motorcycle roared into our driveway.

"Who on earth!" cried Mom, as a tall man wearing low slung jeans and a heavily studded leather jacket got off the bike. His shirt, which was open all the way down to his belly button revealed a hairy chest and three tattoos. When he removed his helmet we could see that what little hair he had on his head was long, dark, and tied in a tail.

"He's huge!" gasped Jennifer.

"Must...uh...be for you," Harry said to Mom and went into the dining room. I followed. I felt safer there. Harry set his stack of papers on the table, got out his pen and began writing. Then the doorbell rang. I stuck my head out the dining room doorway. I could see Jennifer standing in the entryway next to the staircase. I heard Mom open the door.

"Yes?" Mom said.

"Hell-looooooo!" I heard the man say in a voice that was as big as he was. "Now I just kno-ooooooow that you are the beeee-yoooo-teeee-ful Sooo-saaaaan!"

"Pardon?" squeaked Mom.

"Are you or are you not the bee-yoo-tee-ful Soosan?"

"And just who wants to know?" asked Mom in a very small high-pitched voice.

"Your ever lovin' *Parrrrr-teeeeee A-neee-MAL!*" cried the man as he thumped his hairy, decorated chest.

I heard the door slam and the lock turned and then I saw Mom run for the back door and heard her lock and bolt it.

The front doorbell rang again. Mom went into the living room and stood in the middle of the room with her cupped hands over her mouth. Harry kept on writing. He didn't seem to hear anything! The doorbell rang again. And again. And again. Harry kept on writing. Mom finally threw her shoulders back, took a deep breath and went to the door. This time I followed.

"Look!" Mom yelled through the closed door. "I don't know you and I don't want to know you. Now please go away!"

"Hey lady! You want to par-teeee and I am your man! Let's go! Just look at those wheels! Ever see anything like them? That's *pow-er*, Baby. *POWER!* Now get your glad rags on and we'll hit the road, *together.*"

"Go away or I'll call the police!" screeched Mom.

"Hey, Babe. It was *you* said you wanted to party."

"What are you talking about?" gasped Mom. "I didn't say I wanted to party. I don't even know you."

I turned around and looked at Jennifer. She was standing behind me, at the foot of the stairs, her face white and frozen looking. "Don't let her kill me, Pip," she whispered.

"That's what the computer's for, Darlin'" the man yelled through the door, "to get us party animals together."

I could *feel* Jennifer shaking.

"Computer?" asked Mom, her voice oddly quiet. "What computer?"

"The Dating Service."

Jennifer hit the stairs running. I heard her door slam and something very heavy scraping the floor.

Mom opened the door and stared at the man. "What dating service?"

"Look, Darlin'. I filled out the questionnaire and you filled out the questionnaire. The computer did the rest."

"You must be mistaken," Mom said, her voice trembling and her face turning a shade yellow. "I didn't fill out any questionnaire."

"Course you did! I saw it. I read it. You *love* to party! So do I!"

"Sir, there has been a terrible mistake," gasped Mom. "I really did *not* fill out any questionnaire, any form, any anything. Someone must have been playing a trick on me."

"You don't like to party?"

"No," gasped Mom, her hand at her throat. "I definitely do not. I'm sorry for the inconvenience, Mr.—"

"Joe. Just call me Joe. You sure about this, now?"

"Positive."

"Well, if you're sure, I'm sorry to be botherin' ya. It looked real good there, for a moment. Be seein' ya." He looked at me and saluted. "See ya Guy," he said and ambled out to his bike. As he roared out of the driveway, he saluted again.

"He was kind of nice, Mom."

Mom closed the door, locked it, and leaned against it, breathing hard. Then she looked up the stairs. "*JENNIFER!*" she screamed and ran up the steps. I followed. Mom's face was pink, now. She banged on Jennifer's door. "*JENNIFER!*" She pushed against the door. It wouldn't open. "Jennifer, whatever you've got piled in front of this door, you'd better move, *now.*" There was no sound. "All right, Jennifer, *stay there!*"

Mom's face was red, now. "You're grounded forever! *Forever!* You cannot ever, ever, *ever* come out of your room. You'll stay there until you're old, until you're *grey,* until you're *wrinkled,* and need a *cane!* You understand, Jennifer? Do I make myself *clear?*"

There was no sound.

Mom's face was kind of purpley now, as she slumped down the stairs and into the kitchen. I followed. I wondered what Jennifer was doing. I figured she was either hiding under her bed or in the closet. I was sure she wasn't crying.

Mom poured a cup of coffee and flopped down in a chair. "What I don't understand," she said, "is how on earth he got my address."

Suddenly I remembered the phone call about the survey. I guess that's why Joe had saluted me. He knew it was me who'd given him the address. I decided Mom didn't need me anymore and I slunk into the dining room. Harry was still writing.

Chapter Twelve

WHEN JENNIFER'S LOST CAUSE WAS FOUND

"It's all over," groaned Jennifer. "All over." I was getting sick of hearing it. That was all Jennifer had been able to say for three days, now. "All, all over. All that time. All that work. All that planning. *All that money!* Gone." She sighed. Can't say I didn't give it my best shot, though."

"Come on, Jen," I begged. "Play catch with me. Mom said I could join baseball this year. I need to practice." I grabbed her arm and tried to pull her off the back porch. She wouldn't budge. I pulled harder.

"Yarowww!"

Jennifer stood up and I, still pulling on her arm, fell over backwards onto the grass. We both looked towards the garage. Fluffy was sitting on the corner of the roof gazing intently at Spike. Spike was gazing hungrily at Fluffy.

"Yarowwww!" growled Fluffy, and he spit.

Spike bounded over to the fence, then stood and stared, unblinking, at Fluffy. Fluffy, with one last spit, ambled back inside, through the open window.

"Okay," said Jennifer. "Show's over. Let's play catch." We played catch. "Why don't I pitch and you bat?" suggested Jennifer.

I got the bat and stood in the driveway near the fence. That way, when Jennifer threw a bad pitch, the fence would stop it and I wouldn't have to chase it. Jennifer threw a lot of bad pitches. Each time a ball hit the fence Spike would glance over at us. It made me nervous. After a while Spike got used to the balls and grew tired waiting for Fluffy to re-appear. He laid down and went to sleep, by the fence, by the garage.

"Oh, oh," whispered Jennifer, keeping the ball. "Look."

I looked. Fluffy was creeping out of the window. Mom came out just then carrying a big basket of laundry.

"Shhhhh!" I whispered and pointed towards Fluffy and Spike. We all watched, holding our breath, as Fluffy edged over to the corner of the garage roof. Spike slept on. Then suddenly Fluffy sprang, all claws bared, and landed on Spike's back. Spike screamed and bolted. Fluffy hung on. Spike, yelping pitifully, and Fluffy growling murderously, rounded the corner of the house.

Mrs. Agatha Spencer trotted out her back door. "Spikey!" she cried. "My poor baby!"

At the sound of her voice, Spike turned and headed for the back porch, his pathetic yelping and howling sliced the air. As he leapt over the porch railing, Fluffy let go. Spike rushed through the door, and as Mrs. Agatha Spencer yelled insults at us, Fluffy pranced back, head and tail held high.

"Well," laughed Mom. "That just shows there's no such thing as a lost cause."

"*Really*, Mom?" Jennifer asked.

"I may have let you out of your room for a little fresh air, young lady, but I'm still not speaking to you," Mom said, but she was grinning.

I could only stare at Mom. What she'd said! And Jennifer had 'that look' again! "Jennifer!" I cried in desperation. "*This is a lost cause, okay?*"

"But, Pip! There's just got to be a way!"

"Just pitch, Jen!"

Mom began hanging up the towels. Jennifer pitched. I swung and HIT!

"A high fly ball to left field," announced Jennifer in her announcer's voice. "And look at him run!" she continued. "Well, *run*, Pip. You have to run the bases. Don't you know *anything*?"

"We don't have bases, Jen."

"Pretend!" she shouted. I ran. "Rounding second, now third… It's a home run!" screamed Jennifer.

"Nice hit, young fella."

We all whirled around. A tall, overweight man dressed in navy shorts and a spotlessly clean white collared tee shirt was standing there. We hadn't even noticed his big black Chrysler enter the driveway, which shows what a big mouth Jennifer has.

"He must be *loaded*," breathed Jennifer.

"Jennifer!" I groaned.

"How do you do," he said to Mom. "I'm looking for—"

And that's when all the computer dating stuff, the phone calls, the letters, and everything else Jennifer had thrown at Mom, caught up to her. That's when Mom flipped out!

"Looking for fun!" cried Mom, striding towards the man, a towel in her hand. "That it? PAR-TY! Well just get this straight *right now*, buster," yelled Mom, coming right up to the man and pushing her face almost into his. "*I don't like par-tee!*" The man, eyes popping, stepped backwards as Mom continued to advance. "Got it? Well, repeat it so I know you know: *SUSAN MILLER does not like to PAR-TEE!*" She swatted the towel through the air and the man stumbled backwards and fell. "*REPEAT IT!*" she screamed, standing over the obviously terrified man. "*NO PARTEE! NO FUN!*"

"Hi…uh…Davey," called Harry from his window.

Mom stopped. Her towel slumped to the ground, and for a moment I thought she might follow it. "What?" she said, in a very quiet voice.

"I was looking for Harrison," the man said as he got up and dusted himself off.

"Harry?" squeaked Mom.

"Yes," the man said. "I'm his accountant."

"Oh, my goodness," groaned Mom. She sat down on the back step and put her head in her hands.

"Mom?" Jennifer asked. "Would you like me to hang up the towels for you?"

Mom slowly raised her head and stared at Jennifer for a full minute before the glazed look in her eyes disappeared. *"Jennifer!"* Jennifer ran into the house. "I told you to stay in your room forever. *Forever!* Is that *clear*?"

Jennifer stuck her head out her bedroom window. "Yes, Mom. Perfectly clear. You sure you don't want me to hang up the towels?"

"Jennifer!" Mom said, her voice loud, but steady. "I have *never, never, ever, been so completely and massively embarrassed in my entire life!*"

Jennifer shut her window.

Mom hung the towels, then went inside and I soon heard the vacuum. I found my ball and began bouncing it off the wall. Harry had promised to play ball with me that evening and Harry never broke a promise. Not ever. Unless he forgot.

The man Harry had called Davey came down the steps carrying a bag full of papers.

"Is that Harry's book?" I asked.

"No, these are Harrison's receipts," the man replied. "His file, unfortunately, is the floor, the kitchen drawers, the waste basket, vegetable crisper, and anything else that does not resemble a file."

"Oh."

A window went up. The man and I both looked up as Jennifer stuck her head out.

"I'm sorry, sir." She said.

I stared. *Sir?* What was coming, now?

"It's all my fault. Because of me, my mother thought you were someone else. A simple case of mistaken identity which I hope you can forgive."

"Oh, that's all right," the man said, smiling just a little.

"She's really a very nice person."

"Yes, well I'm sure she is," said the man, going towards his car.

"Really, really nice."

"Uh-huh," said the man. He opened the back door and tossed Harry's papers on the back seat.

"Can you come in for a cup of coffee?"

"Oh, I don't think that would be a good idea."

"And a donut? Mom bought groceries today. They're jelly donuts."

"Sounds delicious, but I really don't think your mother would appreciate my company."

"*Mom!*" screeched Jennifer. The vacuum stopped. "Mom, you want to give this gentleman some coffee and a jelly donut, don't you? It's the least you can do, right?"

Mom came out on the porch and glared at Jennifer. Then she turned to the man and I could see her face getting all red again. But it wasn't a mad red this time. It was an embarrassed red. All blotchy kind of.

"Please do come in, Mr...?"

"Brown," said the man. "David Brown."

"How do you do," said Mom. "I'm Susan Miller. Please do forgive me. I thought you were someone else. It's been an unbelievable few days. Do come in and have a coffee and a donut and let me explain"

"Well..."

"As my daughter says, it's the very least I can do."

"Why thank you, Susan," David said, smiling. "I'd be delighted."

I stared in disbelief as they disappeared into the kitchen. But there was no kitchen table anymore. I wondered if they'd go into the living room, the dining room, or just lean against the kitchen counter.

"*See?*" crowed Jennifer. I looked up. She was grinning smugly. "There really aren't any lost causes. And get a load of that car, would ya! Must have cost a bundle or two!"

"Play…uh…ball!"

I whirled around and there was Harry carrying two old shirts and wearing a baseball cap.

"That's first," said Harry, throwing one shirt down. "That's… uh…third," he said, tossing the other one. "And the tree'll be…uh… second. Ready? Batter up! Oh, I forgot…uh…something." He took his cap off and tossed it down next to me. "That's…uh…home."

And Harry could pitch! And he could catch! And he showed me how to hold the bat, how to stand to swing the bat and I actually hit a lot of balls. Then Harry showed me how to hold my gloved hand to catch a pop fly, and how to hold it for grounders. He hit a few balls to me and I actually caught some of them. I caught one pop fly and two grounders! But the line drive hit me, instead.

"Pip! Are you hurt?" cried Harry as he ran towards me. "Sorry, Buddy," he said, when he looked down on my contorted body. "I got carried…uh…away. You're so good I forgot you…uh…were just learning."

"I'm good?" I gasped, through clenched stomach muscles.

"Amazingly good! I…uh…wonder what kind of…uh…game they play in Erpzig…uh…Land. Can you get up Pip?" Harry asked. "Well, at least you can…uh…breathe." After another minute he helped me to stand and walk back to the porch.

"I'm okay, Harry," I said, rubbing my belly.

"Honest?"

"Honest."

"Uh...sure?"

"Sure."

"If you're sure, I ...uh...gotta go! They play...uh...*Smookies* in Erpzig!" And Harry ran for the garage stairs.

Jennifer opened her window again. "Guess what?" she asked, grinning.

"What?" I asked, not at all certain I really wanted to know.

"Mom's not mad at me, anymore."

"Then how come you're still in your room?"

"Because she hasn't gotten around to telling me yet."

"Then how do you know, Jennifer?" I asked, wishing I hadn't. But she didn't say it was because she was a girl. She just grinned.

"Always remember, Pip," she said. "There's no such thing as a lost cause."

"*What?*"

"Sssssh! They're coming."

"Who's coming?"

"Mom and David."

"Mom and—"

And Mom and David did come. Out the front door. And they were laughing! David went to his car and opened his door. "Seven twenty-five?" he called back.

"Seven twenty-five," Mom answered. David drove off. Mom just stood there by the driveway, at the other end of the house watching him drive away. And she was grinning!

"What's seven twenty-five?" I whispered to Jennifer.

"Their date!" Jennifer whispered back. Then she turned her head towards Mom and called, "Hi Mom!"

"Oh, hi, Jennifer," Mom replied. She was still grinning. "What are you doing up in your room on such a beautiful day?"

What was she doing up in her room? "But you—" I started to say.

"Quiet!" whispered Jennifer. "Nothing, Mom. You want me for something?"

"Well, maybe you could set the table for me. We're eating early. And Pip, could you see if Harry could come over tonight? I need a sitter and Jeff can't come."

I looked up at Jennifer. She was grinning down at me. "Girls just know these things," she whispered.

Chapter Thirteen

WHEN JENNIFER WISHED HER LOST CAUSE WAS STILL LOST

When I heard the Chrysler pull into our driveway, I slipped out of bed and snuck out into the darkened hall. I bumped into Jennifer. We huddled near the top of the stairs and waited. And waited.

"Do you suppose he's kissing her?" Jennifer asked in an excited whisper.

My stomach went all flippity. I didn't want to think about it.

"Sssh. She's coming," whispered Jennifer when we heard steps on the porch. The key turned and Mom came in and leaned against the closed door. She was smiling to herself and looked all funny peculiar. "He did!" whispered Jennifer, squeezing my hand. "He did kiss her!"

I almost asked how she knew that but stopped myself just in time.

Harry came into the hallway. "Hi," he said.

"What's *he* doing here?" whispered Jennifer, angrily.

"He's the *babysitter*!" I reminded her.

"Oh. Right."

"Hi, Harry," said Mom. She took off her coat and Harry hung it up for her.

"What's he doing that for?" asked Jennifer. "He never does stuff like that."

"Yes, he does," I declared. "When he's not working."

"He does? Really?"

"Yah, he does."

"Oh." She sounded disappointed.

Mom sat on the second from the bottom step. "How'd you and the kids get along?" she asked.

"Uh…fine," said Harry, sitting down next to her. "Fine. You have…uh…great kids."

"Yes, I do. Thank you."

Jennifer poked me and I smiled in the dark and poked her back.

"Have a good time," asked Harry, "with…uh…Davey?"

Mom nodded. "We went to this fabulous restaurant. French! There were things on that menu I'd never heard of!"

"Told you she liked to have fun," whispered Jennifer. I glared at her, but the effect was undoubtedly lost in the dark.

"And the waiter was so perfect. He made me feel like a princess."

"What money can do!" crowed Jennifer.

"I'm …uh…glad," said Harry, but I didn't think his voice sounded glad.

"And we danced."

"Davey a good…uh…dancer?"

"Mmmm quite good," said Mom. "A little stiff, though."

"Accountants," said Harry, "well, accountants…uh…just are."

Mom laughed. "I guess so."

"Like him?" asked Harry.

"Oh, yes, I suppose. He's very nice, just—"

"A little…uh…stiff."

Mom laughed.

"I wonder," whispered Jennifer, "how you go about un-stiffening someone."

"Jen!" I had to cover my mouth with both hands to keep from laughing out loud.

"Going to see him…uh…again?" Harry asked.

"Yes, actually. On Wednesday. At eight-oh-seven."

"Eight-oh-*seven*?" asked Harry.

"Funny, isn't it," laughed Mom. "I guess he's very punctual."

"Well…uh…accountants are."

"Is he a good accountant?"

"Must be. He…uh…yells at me enough."

"Do you like him, Harry?"

"Yah. Davey's…uh…okay. He's just a little—"

"Stiff," supplied Mom and they both laughed again.

"Well, I guess I'll be on my…uh…way."

"I was thinking, Harry, about your bills and things."

"I always…uh…forget."

"Hah!" whispered Jennifer. "Doesn't have the money, he means."

"Does, too," I hissed.

"I know, Harry," said Mom. "But in return for sitting the kids—"

"Don't…uh…worry about it. The pleasure's all…uh…mine."

"No, really. I know you won't accept money—"

"Why not," whispered Jennifer. "He obviously needs it."

"Ssssh! I want to hear!"

"Of course I can't accept…uh…money!" cried Harry.

"Well, I thought maybe I could return the favour. I might be going on a few dates in the future and I'll need a sitter and I really don't feel Jeff is that reliable."

"I'm…uh…always available."

"Wonderful! And I thought I could keep track of your bills and make out the cheques and mail them for you. You'd just have to sign them."

"And watch them bounce," snickered Jennifer.

"Jen!"

"You'd...uh...do that?"

"Certainly," replied Mom. "No problem."

"My wife...uh...used to do that, too," said Harry.

"*Wife*!" Jennifer and I gasped together.

"You're married, Harry?" asked Mom, apparently as surprised as we were.

"I was. We're...uh...divorced."

"Is *everyone* divorced?" I whispered to Jennifer.

"Join the club," said Mom. "Not easy, is it?"

Harry shook his head. "Well, I better...uh...go. You sure you don't mind?"

"Not at all. It's nothing compared to sitting."

"That's nothing compared to...uh...paying bills and things," Harry said as he stood up. "I love your kids."

Smiling, I went back to bed, and after that Mom and David went out every Saturday and every Wednesday. Sometimes it was at six twenty-five, or seven forty-nine or even eight fifty-one.

"How come he doesn't just say eight o'clock or seven-thirty, then get here a little early or a little late like everybody else?" I asked Harry one Saturday.

"Well, Pip, it's because...uh...well, it's because he's...uh...an accountant. That's why."

"Oh."

On the second Wednesday Mom wasn't quite ready when David arrived at six forty-seven. "Sorry, David," Mom said when she came down. "We had a little accident."

"You must learn to schedule your time, Susan," declared David, tightening his tie and opening the door.

"Oh, I do, David," said Mom. "If I didn't we'd never survive. However, you can't schedule scraped knees."

"I'm sure you could if you tried, Susan," David said, glaring at me and my bandaged knee. Mom laughed. David didn't.

"Well, let's be on our way, shall we?" said David, glaring at me again. We'll have to rush, now, I'm afraid. *We're late.*"

"See ya, Davey," Harry called.

"Right, Harrison," said David.

"He wasn't joking about scheduling scraped knees, was he, Harry?" I asked as we watched them drive away.

"No, Pip, I don't think he…uh…was."

"How do you schedule them, Harry?"

"You…uh…can't."

"Then how come he—"

"He's…uh…an accountant, Pip."

"Oh. Harry?"

"Yah?"

"How come David doesn't allow the rest of us to call him Davey like you do?"

"He doesn't…uh…allow me, either, Pip. I just…uh…do it."

"How come he doesn't get mad at you when you call him that? He gets mad at me."

"Oh, he…uh…does, Pip. He does."

"He does? But I've never heard him get mad at you like he does me."

"Well, that's…uh…because he doesn't dare."

"Because you'll beat up on him? Or throw things? Like you and Dr. Wiggins?"

Harry laughed. "No. I doubt that has ever crossed his…uh…mind."

"Why then?"

"Because I'm his client. And he's afraid if he said…uh…anything that I'd get a different…uh…accountant. And money is everything to…uh…Davey."

I screwed up my face. This was getting complicated. "You mean *he* works for *you*?"

"Right. And others."

I couldn't understand that. If David worked *for* Harry, then how come it was David who had all the money? Mom worked *for* her boss but she sure didn't have all the money!

"Come on, Pip," said Harry. "Let's practice your…uh…hitting and leave Davey and your mother to…uh…each other."

"Harry?"

"Yes, Pip?"

"If it makes David mad to be called Davey, how come you do it?"

"That's why. Because it makes him…uh…mad. He's what one might call pompous, and pompous…uh…annoys me."

"Oh." I wished I had the courage to call him Davey, but once was enough.

The weeks became routine. Mom's and David's dates continued to be every Wednesday and Saturday. My baseball games were every Monday and Wednesday. Mom, Harry and Jennifer came with me on Mondays. Harry and Jennifer came on Wednesdays. I invited David to a game on Wednesday so Mom could come then, too.

"I don't like baseball," David said.

"Oh," I said. *He didn't like baseball!*

On the fourth Saturday, David glared at me again. "You shouldn't have your Lego in the living room," he said.

"Why not?" I asked.

"Because it's messy," David informed me. *He thinks Lego is messy!* "Living rooms should always be immaculate."

"Imma—?"

"Immaculate," repeated David. "In perfect order. Nothing out of place. Not a speck of dust anywhere." David rubbed a finger over a lampshade, looked at it, glowered, and hastily pulled out a hanky and wiped his finger off. "Not a speck." He repeated.

"Why?" I asked.

In case guests arrive."

"But guests could go in there," I said, pointing to the den. "This is the *living* room."

David sighed, and as Mom came down the stairs, beautiful in a pale blue dress, David looked at his watch. "It's seven thirty-*nine*," he said, glowering at Mom. How could anyone that beautiful be glowered at? I wondered. I wished I was older. I wished I was old enough to tell David to get out and not to come back, but Mom just laughed and kissed me good-bye. It didn't seem to have bothered her at all.

"See ya, Davey," Harry called as they went out the door.

David stopped long enough to glower at Harry and then slammed the door.

"Isn't this the *living* room, Harry?" I asked.

"He's...uh...an accountant, Pip."

"Give it a rest, Pip," Jennifer said when I complained to her. "Think of all the good things. The car, the toys, the clothes, the trips, the *Barbies*."

"But what good are toys if you can't play with them?"

"Oh, don't be silly, Pip. You can play with then in your room."

"But then I'd miss my television programs, and being with Mom."

"But then you'll have a television in your room."

"Oh." I hadn't thought of that. "Will Mom and Harry be in my room, too?"

"Of course not! Don't be silly! David will be here then."

"*In my room?*" I screeched.

"Of course not! Jeepers, Pip."

The next Saturday, David glowered at Jennifer. "Turn that thing down!" he said. Jennifer stared at him, blankly. "Your music! You can't hear yourself think. You'll ruin your ears and your brain will turn to mush!" Jennifer looked at the stereo and then at David.

"Turn it *off*!" he cried. Jennifer pressed a button and glared at David, but David was looking at Mom coming down the stairs. "It's six *eleven*!" he said.

"We're just going to have to put a stop to this," sighed Jennifer as we went out to the back yard.

"What?" I asked.

"Well, David is just so…so…"

"Uh…unreasonable?" suggested Harry.

"Right. Unreasonable. Talk to her, Harry."

"Uh…talk to her?"

"Yah. You and Mom are always having conversations after dates, so why not tell her what you think?"

"I think it's none of my…uh…business," said Harry. He was staring at the old Chestnut. "You know, when I was a kid I had a tree like…uh…this one."

"But don't you feel responsible? He's your accountant."

"Uh…no."

"But Harry," argued Jennifer, "listen. It really is your business. You live here, too."

"Not if they get…uh…married," said Harry.

"*What*?" we gasped, together..

"Couldn't," said Harry. "I had a tree house in my…uh…tree."

"But why not?" I cried.

"But I…uh…did," Harry said. "A really neat…uh…tree house."

"He means why couldn't you stay here if they got married?" Jennifer said as though she was explaining it to a little kid."

"Just couldn't, that's all," said Harry. "Let's build a…uh…tree house."

"With what?" asked Jennifer.

"Uh…lumber."

"We don't have any," Jennifer said, still in that explaining tone of hers.

"I'll get…uh…some."

"Can you afford it?" asked Jennifer, screwing up her face.

"Probably. We could…uh…check with your mother or Davey, but they aren't …uh…here." He walked under the tree, and all around it. "Pip, go see if…uh…my bank books are there."

"Where?"

"Uh…desk? Maybe a cupboard drawer? I don't know. You'll…uh…find them."

"See you sometime next week, Pip," Jennifer called after me.

"And a pen and paper and…uh…tape measure." called Harry.

"Never mind that stuff, Pip," called Jennifer. "I'll get ours, or we might never see you again."

I ran into the apartment and began my search. A tree house! I could hardly believe it. I waded through the wads of paper and the piles of clothes, gave Fluffy a cuddle, and began investigating Harry's desk. There were several pads of paper on top of the desk and there were dozens of pens and pencils in the middle drawer. But the cheque book was no where to be found.

I fed Fluffy and then began searching the kitchen. It was not that difficult. Except for a few essentials like crackers, bread, and peanut butter, the cupboards were all but empty. The drawers were a different matter. Besides cutlery, there were letters, crumpled bits of paper, socks, dirty socks, and underwear. And there was nothing but dust and one letter on top of the fridge.

I opened the fridge. Jam. Mustard. Pickles. I opened the crisper and quickly closed it again for fear some of whatever it was, might jump out and get me. I opened the butter keeper and was amazed to discover butter.

Then I opened the meat keeper. Below some greenish bologna was a brown envelope with BANK BOOKS written on it in Mom's big bold printing. I took the envelope out and dumped the contents on the counter top. There were three books and a typewritten sheet with a bunch of words and numbers on it.

I recognized the cheque book because it was the same as Mom's. I opened it to the last entry. The balance read five hundred and seventy three dollars and twenty-nine cents. And the rent was due in a few days! Maybe Harry couldn't afford the tree house. I sighed. It would have been so neat!

Then I opened one of the other books. I stared at the last entry. But this just couldn't be! This was impossible! I looked at the date. The date was last month. A withdrawal. And the balance read seventy three thousand, two hundred and ninety six dollars and forty-seven cents! I flopped onto the floor and opened the last book. "Jen!" I whispered when I looked at the figures. "Oh, Jen, are you going to be surprised!" I stared and stared at the figures but they didn't change and they didn't disappear. Two hundred and twelve thousand, two hundred and sixty-one dollars and fifteen cents!

Oh my gosh! Oh my gosh! I couldn't think. My head was spinning. I stuffed the contents back into the envelope and started for the door. "Jen!"

Then I stopped. And then I smiled.

I went back to the counter and emptied the envelope. Then I put the savings books back inside, glanced at the typewritten page which said something about bonds and stuffed it back inside. I took the cheque book and headed for the door. I walked down the steps. I walked very, very, slowly. I needed time to practice not grinning.

I handed the book to Harry. He glanced inside and said," Yep, I can write a…uh…cheque." I had to bite my lips. I had to bite them *hard* to keep from grinning.

"You okay, Pip?" Jennifer asked.

I bit so hard I yelped and had to rub my lips. "Yah," I said from behind my hand. "I'm fine, Jen."

Harry went over to the tree and climbed up onto the first branch and began to measure.

"Do you think Mom's going to marry David?" Jennifer asked.

"No," I said.

"You don't?"

"No," I repeated, biting my lip again.

"Well, I'm not so sure," said Jennifer. "And he can be such a pain, sometimes. I don't know what it would be like if he was around *all* the time. I mean, just imagine having *breakfast* with him every morning!"

I bit my lip again.

"And if Harry moved..." continued Jennifer, sighing. "Well, I don't know. He's a genuine nut case, but..."

"He's not an accountant," I supplied.

"Right," agreed Jennifer, smiling up at Harry, who was now dangling from an upper branch. "That about sums it up, I guess. You know, Pip, I think I'd even miss Harry if he left."

"Don't worry, Jen," I said. "He's *not* going to move."

"Yah, and how do *you* know that?"

"Sometimes," I said, grinning now even though I was biting hard, "sometimes boys just know these things!"

Jennifer scowled at me. Then she burst out laughing. "Oh, Pip! Get real!"

Chapter Fourteen

WHEN JENNIFER WOULD HAVE BEEN PROUD OF ME

My mind had been working lickety-split, non-stop. Somehow, I was going to have to show Harry that he was right for Mom and show Mom that she was right for Harry. And I was going to do it all without telling Jennifer a single thing.

"Mom really likes those talks you have when she gets home from a date," I told Harry when I saw him. Harry was working on a painting for his book.

"Oh?"

"Yah. She told me." Mom hadn't told me, but still, I knew, I just knew, I wasn't lying.

"Oh?" repeated Harry.

"That's the best part of the evening, she said."

"Oh?" said Harry. "What do you…uh…think? Too much purple?"

Harry hadn't heard a word I'd said. But did it matter? The little boy's mother had begun to appear in the paintings of Erpzigland. And she looked an awful lot like Mom. I smiled and started out.

But still, I thought, the little boy needs a father. I turned back. "He needs a father, Harry."

Harry looked up. Harry had heard me! "What?" asked Harry.

"Your boy. In Erpzigland. He really needs a father."

"You…uh…think?"

"Yah. I think."

"Well.…Maybe you're…uh…right. I'll have to think about that. I thought I'd give him a…uh…sister."

"Not necessary," I declared.

"No?"

"No."

"Well.…No, I think there should be a big…uh…sister. It feels right. I think that's…uh…what's been missing."

"He needs a father, Harry. A really nice father."

"Uh…maybe."

"One who plays Smookies with him."

"Uh…right. Smookies. Maybe you're…uh…right."

I left. It was enough for now.

When I saw Jennifer I suggested she and I eat in the living room that night.

"The living room? Why? I like the dining room. I'm even glad I sold the kitchen table. It's nice in there. And, thanks to me, we get to eat there every day. Even breakfast!"

"But this way we could eat and watch television at the same time."

"Mom will never let us."

"If she'll let us, will you?"

"Okay. Sure."

I found Mom. "Can Jen and I eat in the living room and watch cartoons?"

"Oh, Pip! What a thought! It'd give me indigestion."

"Not you, Mom. Just Jen and me."

"Oh, I hardly think so. You watch enough junk without doing it at mealtime."

"But you'd get some peace and quiet. You wouldn't have to listen to Jennifer."

Mom laughed. "That is tempting, Pip, but I'd still hear the cartoons. I think that'd be worse."

"We'll turn it down low. And we could put some music on in the dining room. You wouldn't hear the TV or Jennifer." Mom squinched up her face. "Just this once, Mom. Please!"

"All right, but just this once!"

"Great! Thanks Mom! And I'll set the table for you."

"Aren't you sweet! Thank you, Pip."

I set two places. I used the woven mats and the good china. I opened a drawer in the china cabinet and got out the good silverware and the silver napkin rings. I opened another drawer and found a candle holder and a candle. I put everything on the table, then ran outside and picked some pink flowers and put them in a blue vase, and set them on the table. I stood back and looked. I was almost positive that it looked nice.

I hurried over to Harry's apartment and waded through the paper to where Harry was sitting at his art table, scowling at his painting. I looked. Harry had drawn in a father for the boy. The father was tall. He was dark haired. He had a pot belly. He was wearing *a business suit! He was David!*

"*Harry!*" I cried.

"Uh...not right, is it?" said Harry.

"*NO!*"

Harry crumpled up the page, tossed it on the floor with the other discards and rolled out another piece from the big roll of paper that was attached to the top of his art table.

"Just a sister, then," sighed Harry.

"Harry, no!" I groaned.

"Yup. Just a mother and a big sister. Now…sister…big sister…let me…uh…think." And Harry drew Jennifer.

I sighed. This was not going to be easy! "It's time for supper," I said.

"Oh, is it?" asked Harry, getting up and scrunching across the floor. "I didn't know. Actually, I…uh…never know."

"How about changing your clothes, Harry?" I suggested. "These are all painty."

"Are they?" he asked, and looked down at himself.

"And your toes are sticking our of your shoes."

He looked down again. "Uh…so they are."

"So, change."

He looked at the clothes lying on his floor, then looked in the closet. Empty hangers hung from the rod. He turned back to the floor and picked up a pair of pants.

"They're all painty, too," I said.

"Uh…so they are. Well…I don't see…uh…anything else. Must be time to do the…uh…laundry."

"No, Harry," I said, using the firmest voice ever. "It's time to go shopping."

"Shopping?"

"Yes, Harry. Shopping." I looked around. "But also laundry. Got a bag?"

He found a big garbage bag in the bathroom where the towels were supposed to be, and kicking through the crumpled papers, digging under the bed, and looking into boxes and kitchen drawers, we filled the bag with Harry's laundry.

"I'll do it for you, Harry."

"You…uh… will?"

"Sure, but only if you go shopping for new clothes tomorrow."

"I don't know, Pip. I'm not very good at…uh…shopping. Will you come with me?"

"Sure!"

"But I need to check with...uh...David to see if I can afford—"

"You can, Harry. I checked with Mom already." I hadn't, so that was a lie, but I did know he could afford to do this, so that wasn't a lie, so I hoped that was somehow okay.

"Sure?"

"Trust me."

"Okay, Buddy, we'll go!" He picked up the bag of laundry and followed me over to our house. While Harry put the bag in the laundry room, I carried supper into the dining room.

"Oh, isn't it lovely!" cried Mom, as she sat down across from Harry.

"Light the candle, Harry." I said.

Harry lit the candle, but the sun was shining in the window and it didn't show up. I hadn't thought of that. All that showed up was the paint on Harry's clothes. And the holes. I hadn't thought of that, either.

"Oh, this is beautiful, Pip," cried Mom. Well, it had the right effect on one person, anyway, I thought. "But I should have cooked something more special," she groaned. "Somehow macaroni and franks don't go with the silver."

I hadn't thought of that, either. It was like Jennifer said, I just didn't think. I would definitely have to do better!

Jennifer came in, looked at the table and screwed up her face at me. I shrugged my shoulders and began dishing up my supper.

"Aren't you two...uh...eating with us?"

"No, we're eating in the living room and watching cartoons," replied Jennifer.

"*Cartoons!*" cried Harry. And he picked up his plate and dashed into the living room, leaving Mom alone at the table.

This was definitely not going to be easy, I thought, as I followed Harry. I could hardly concentrate on the cartoons for wondering what I could possibly do to bring out the romantic side of Harry. I continued to wonder all the next morning while Jennifer and I watched Harry work on our tree house. But no magical ideas came. No bolt of lightning to solve all my problems.

"There!" Harry called down to us after a couple of hours work. "How's…uh… that for a floor?" He jumped up and down. "Good and…uh…strong!"

"Great!" I cried. This was getting exciting.

"And he did it with only a couple of bangs to his thumb and three or four bandages," commented Jennifer.

"It was only two bandages and you know it!" I said.

"Whatever. Can we come up now, Harry?"

"Nope."

"Why not?"

"Because there's…uh…nothing to keep you from…uh…falling off," he said, as he climbed down the ladder.

"Ah, come on, Harry!" Jennifer exclaimed. "We're not babies!"

"I know, Jennifer, but that's the…uh…rule."

"Oh, fudgie!"

"It's getting kinda late, Harry," I said.

"Late for…uh…what?" asked Harry.

"Yah, Pip, late for what?" asked Jennifer.

"Shopping."

"*Shopping?*"

"Pip says I need some…uh…clothes," said Harry, looking a little embarrassed.

"Gee, I wonder what gave him that idea?" asked Jennifer. "Can I come?"

"*NO!*" I cried.

"Why not?" they asked together.

"Because this is *man stuff.*"

"It is not," declared Jennifer, with her hands on her hips. "There's no such thing."

"I...uh...think she's probably right, Pip."

"Well, it's..." I stammered. I just *couldn't* let Jennifer come! "It's...Well you said you'd make supper, Jen, and we won't be back in time."

"Oh, fudgie! Go then! See if I care!" She stuck her tongue out at me.

"Okay, let's...uh...go!" said Harry.

"You need your wallet, Harry," I reminded him, and Harry trotted off to his apartment.

"Are you sure he can afford to go shopping, Pip?" asked Jennifer. "I mean, it'd be awful if you made him spend all this money on clothes and then he got into trouble. Like if he couldn't pay his *rent*."

"It's okay, Jen, we checked."

"Well, don't let him go crazy."

"It's *okay*!"

Harry ran down the steps. "Let's go!"

"This is really something for the books," mumbled Jennifer.

"Now, what?" I whined.

"He won't let us up in the tree house, but he lets you in the car when he's driving!"

I ignored her and ran to the car. She had a point, but I wasn't going to tell her that. Driving with Harry was even more fun in the front seat, I thought, as Harry roared backwards into Jeff's driveway and then roared forwards past a stop sign. And it was fun shopping with Harry, too. He loved bright colours: red and orange, green and purple, bright yellow and electric blue. And he discovered sweat suits.

"Where have you been, Harry? I've always had sweat suits."

"What?" asked Harry, bouncing up and down and waving his arms around the dressing room. "Home. I've been at...uh...home. Most of the...uh...time."

Harry bought six sweat suits. There was a black one, a burgundy one, a blue one a navy one, and two grey ones. Some had hoods, some had collars, and some were crew necks. And every one was new. And not one of them had a single drop of paint on it.

"Now jeans, shorts and tees," I said, "and socks and shoes."

"Maybe I'd better…uh…check with your mom…uh…first."

"It's okay, Harry," I assured him, keeping my voice as firm as I could.

"Sure?"

"Sure."

So Harry bought two pairs of jeans, two pairs of cords, four pairs of shorts, six tee shirts, a dozen pairs of socks, a dozen boxers, two pairs of inexpensive sneakers and one very expensive pair.

"I think I should have…uh…checked with your mom," said Harry.

"Everything's fine, Harry. Trust me."

"Sure?"

"Sure. But there is one more thing you need to buy."

"What?"

"Well, think of someone who does a lot for you, Harry."

"You! I need to buy you a…uh…present."

"No. Not me."

Harry thought for a moment. Then he smiled. "Susan!"

We went to the florists and Harry bought Mom a beautiful bouquet of her favourite yellow roses.

"This is wonderful!" cried Harry as we pulled out into the traffic. "I won't have to…uh…shop for ten…uh…years!"

"Yes you will."

"I…uh…will?"

"Yes. And if you don't want to go again next week—"

"I don't!" cried Harry, in alarm.

"Then you have to keep these clothes separate."

"Separate?"

"Yah," I said, with as much authority as I could muster. "See, if you wear anything you want anytime you want, pretty soon everything will have paint on it from working, or be torn from the tree house. Like I keep my Sunday School clothes separate from my play clothes."

"You're very…uh…wise, Pip," said Harry, giving me a swat on the knee and at the same time swerving to miss an oncoming bus.

I glowed. I couldn't help it! I had been *thinking*. If Jennifer knew, she'd be very proud of me. I glowed all the way home. Through the screeching of tires, the angry gestures from pedestrians, and the honking of horns, I glowed.

But Harry was still not certain. "Is it okay, Susan?" he asked, when he showed her all the bags.

"Of course, Harry," Mom replied.

"I thought I should have checked with you…uh…first. I've never bought so much…uh…stuff in my life."

"It's fine," Mom said, and smiled. "I'm glad you did."

"It was all…uh…Pip's idea," he said, smiling at me. "Uh… there's one more thing." Was he really blushing when he handed Mom the roses?

Mom took the roses. She looked at them and then at Harry and then she looked back at the roses. "Thank you, Harry," she whispered. "Now you better put all your purchases away. It's almost suppertime and David will be here at seven twenty-six."

Harry nodded and hurried us out the door, but at the last second I looked back at Mom and I was certain it was her that was glowing now!

Up in Harry's apartment, we laid his new clothes out on his unmade bed. We folded the shorts and tee shirts and placed them in a box and put them in the bottom of his closet. We did the same with his boxers and socks. Then we hung up all his sweat shirts and pants, his jeans and his cords.

"Now promise you won't wear any of these for work, or you'll soon have everything all painty again."

"Uh…right."

"And keep your best sneakers for when you go somewhere."

"Uh…right."

"So don't even open the closet unless you're going to supper or my ball game or something. Okay?" Was I beginning to sound like Jennifer? I shivered at the thought, but I knew it was necessary for my plan to work. And Jennifer *would* be proud of me, if she knew!

When everything was organized, we started down the steps for supper.

"Wait a sec!" exclaimed Harry. "I didn't…uh…change!" We laughed and went back. "This is…uh…closet time, right?" he asked and opened the closet door and chose black cords. "I'll be staying… uh… late, so I better wear a sweat shirt." He looked at all the shirts. "What colour does your…uh…Mom like?"

I grinned. Progress! "Purple," I said, hoping I was right.

So Harry chose the grey sweatshirt with the purple sleeves, and even put on the expensive sneakers without being asked.

"You look great, Harry!" I exclaimed.

"Sure?"

"Sure!"

And he did. Mom said so, too. And Jennifer did, with her face all screwed up in confusion. And even David asked him where his rags were. And that night, when David brought Mom home, I woke up and crawled out onto the landing and listened.

"Where'd you go…uh…tonight?" asked Harry.

"Oh, Harry!" exclaimed Mom, sitting on the step with him. "It was one of the most memorable nights of my life! We went to a play. We saw *Fiddler On The Roof*!"

Harry put his head down. "I didn't even know it was…uh… playing," he said, his voice odd sounding. Like something was hurting him. Like maybe he had a stomach ache.

"Oh, Harry!" cried Mom. "Did you want to go? And you babysat instead? I should have said something! I just didn't think!"

"No, no. I love…uh…babysitting, Susan. It's just that I never know what's…uh…going on. And I…uh…should."

"Of course you know, Harry."

Of course he didn't! What was Mom talking about?

"No, I don't. I'm just not very good at this…uh…reality stuff."

"Harry, you're good at what's important."

Harry shook his head and got up to leave. I could see his face now, dimly reflected in the light from the kitchen.

"I can't even remember to…uh…mail a cheque to pay a bill."

"Mailing a cheque is not what's important in life, Harry. Necessary, I know, but not important."

"A lot of it is…uh…important, Susan." Harry said, sighing. He looked infinitely sad. "My wife always said I'd never hear…uh…the baby cry."

"But most men don't. I don't know a single mother who hasn't said that when the baby cried at night, it was her, not her husband, who heard it."

"I don't mean in the…uh…night, Susan."

Harry swatted himself on the forehead. "I mean in the daytime! When I'm…uh…working!"

"Oh, Harry, of course you would!"

"You think?"

"I *know!*" exclaimed Mom.

"I don't. I really don't! It's…uh…well…it's a frightening…uh…thought."

"Oh, Harry!"

"Gotta go," said Harry, starting down the hall. "I'm really glad you saw…uh…*Fiddler On The Roof* and I'm glad Davey…uh…takes you to those expensive restaurants and…uh…everything. That's where you belong."

"I'm not so sure," said Mom. "Good night, Harry."

"Good night, Susan."

I scurried back into bed. But I didn't pretend to be asleep when Mom came up to check on me. "I really like Harry, Mom," I told her.

"So do I."

"Jennifer says he's a nut case."

Mom laughed. "In a very sweet way, I guess he is."

"But you still like him?" I asked. She smiled and nodded. "He's rich, Mom."

"I know."

"You know?"

"Well, of course he is, Pip. He's written a dozen or more very successful children's novels. Four of them have been made into movies."

"And that makes him rich?"

"Certainly."

"If you know and I know, how come Harry doesn't know?"

"Well, that's a bit difficult to explain, Pip. Deep down I think he does know but he constantly doubts himself when he's dealing with what he terms reality—the day to day goings on of life." I scowled. "Okay, let's see…When you yank Harry away from *his* reality, which is his work, it's like yanking a fish out of water."

I nodded. I understood. Harry lived in a world where the sky was always pink and the trees were always purple. When he looked up and saw that the sky was really blue, it sometimes confused him. "But he's not crazy," I said.

"No," said Mom. "He's just very brilliant. And mainly he's just Harry."

"Good." I said, snuggling down under my covers. "It doesn't really matter, does it?"

"No, Pip, it doesn't matter a bit."

"I didn't think so."

"It only matters if a person is gentle and caring and loving."

I nodded. "Mom, Jennifer doesn't know that Harry's rich. You won't tell her, will you?"

"Not if you don't want me to."

"I don't. It could be dangerous."

"Mmmmm. You're probably right. I won't tell her."

"Thanks, Mom."

"Good night, Pip."

"Good night, Mom." I smiled. Maybe it wouldn't be so difficult, after all. I think I was still smiling when I fell asleep.

Chapter Fifteen

WHEN JENNIFER WANTED HARRY

The next Wednesday, David arrived at five thirty-eight. He and Mom were going to an early supper and a movie.

"I trust, young lady," David said to Jennifer as Mom started down the stairs, "that that mess will not be here when your mother arrives home."

Jennifer looked up from her Barbies and glared at David. Mom stopped half way down the stairs and stared at David.

"This is the *living room*," said David, "not your play room. Your bedroom is for that sort of thing."

Jennifer glared. Mom continued to stare, her face a good deal pinker than it had been at the top of the stairs. I waited and bit my lip to keep from grinning.

"Ready at last, Susan?" David asked.

"Yah, Mom. It's five *forty-one*! Three minutes, *three whole minutes* you've kept this *gentleman* waiting," Jennifer said, her eyes flashing with anger.

"Precisely," said David. "Thank you, Jennifer."

"This has gone *too far*!" fumed Jennifer after they were safely out the door. "We must think of another line of action, Pip."

"Line of action?" I asked.

"*To break them up!*" exclaimed Jennifer. "And what better way to do it than with another man. After all, it's not as though David is rich or anything."

"He's not? But you said—"

"Compared to us, he is. But there's a lot of people with that much money."

"There are?"

"Sure. We just have to find them."

"But it's August already. We don't have time!"

"For what?" asked Jennifer.

"To save the house!"

"Oh. Right. Well, we'll just have to take in boarders. Anything's better than letting Mom marry David." Jennifer thought a moment. "And we could raise Harry's rent. Except he probably couldn't afford it and he'd have to leave."

"We can't let him leave!" I cried.

"Well," thought Jennifer, "at least not until he finishes the tree house."

"*Jennifer!*"

"Well, the biggest priority now—"

"Pri—"

"Priority. The most important thing."

"Oh."

"The biggest priority now is to get rid of David."

"Right," I agreed. I grinned. I couldn't help it. Jennifer was going to help me without even knowing about Harry!

Jennifer plotted and fumed over David all the way to the ball game and all the way back.

"Did you see me catch that grounder?" I cried, as we walked home.

"You were…uh…absolutely terrific!" exclaimed Harry.

"Did you know," growled Jennifer, "that that David actually told me I couldn't have my Barbies in the *living room*?"

"I got on base every time, didn't I, Harry?" I asked, jumping up and down beside him.

"I cheered until I was…uh…hoarse," declared Harry, giving me a squeeze.

"I mean!" said Jennifer. "The nerve!"

"And once, it was even because I hit the ball!"

"I mean," grumbled Jennifer, "like it's *his house* or something!"

"Give it a rest, Jennifer!" I yelled.

"But Pip! The *nerve*! If he's this bad now, what'll he be like when they get married?"

"It's because he's…uh…an accountant." Harry stated.

"My friend's dad is an accountant, Harry, and he's not like that!" Jennifer fumed.

"Well, David…uh…is," Harry declared.

"Right," cried Jennifer, "and we have to do *something*!"

"How about getting…uh…a banana split?" suggested Harry.

"Yay!" I cheered.

"Yah, right, that'll fix everything." And Jennifer continued to fume even while she ate her banana split. And she kept it up the next day. And she plotted.

"Who makes good money, Mom," asked Jennifer.

"My boss."

"Who else?"

"Oh, I don't know. Anyone in management. Depends what you mean by good money."

"More than you."

"Teachers. Nurses."

"Who else, Mom?"

"Jennifer I do not have time for this. I'm going to miss my bus. And you don't have time, either."

"Why not?"

"Because you spend altogether too much time wondering about money and who has how much. It's not healthy. Now, I've got to rush. Don't forget, both of you, to do your chores."

"We won't," we said together.

"And please don't pester Harry. He's there if you need him, but he's having problems pulling his book together and he needs quiet. Just because it's summer holidays doesn't mean you have to be noisy."

"Sure, Mom," said Jennifer. "It's Pip, not me, that bugs him."

"I do not!"

"I have to rush," Mom said, giving us each a kiss. "I'll call at coffee break as usual."

I did my chores and then went over to Harry's. He was staring at his painting. There was a father in it again. It was my baseball coach.

"Not…uh…right, is it?" I shook my head. "There was a man sitting next to me at the…uh…game last night. He seemed like a good…uh…father. I was going to use him. But he got angry when his son…uh…missed a pop fly. And the little guy was trying so…uh…hard, too."

"Oh," I murmured.

"I can't…uh…use him now."

"No."

We sat in silence for a while, staring at the painting. Then I decided I had to take the plunge. I took a deep breath, and jumped in. "Why not use yourself?"

"Oh, no!" cried Harry in obvious alarm. "I couldn't do…uh…that."

"Why not?"

"Because then he'd keep forgetting important…uh…things. Like birthdays and…uh…ball games and swimming lessons. A father shouldn't do…uh…that."

"But the mother could remind him! And the kids! I bet the big sister wouldn't let him forget anything!" Even I could hear the desperation in my voice.

"Well," said Harry. "It might…uh…work."

"Of course it would!"

Harry began to draw himself into the picture. Then suddenly, just as I was about to cheer, he tore the paper off the roll, scrumpled it up and threw it across the room.

"Why'd you do that?" I cried. I could feel my chest tightening and my throat swelling. I jumped out of my chair and ran across the room. I picked up the painting. "It's *good*, Harry. *It's perfect!*"

"No," Harry stated. He pulled down on the paper roll and stared at the blank surface. "No, Pip, it isn't perfect…uh…at all. That father wouldn't…uh…hear the baby cry."

I could feel my insides beginning to shake. "But there *isn't* a baby."

Harry turned and looked straight into my eyes. "There's always…uh…a baby, Pip. Everyone is someone's baby, even if they…uh…live to a hundred and two."

"But, there's no tiny baby!"

"But there…uh…might be, Pip. There might be."

"*There doesn't have to be!*" I cried. My throat was so small now, I couldn't swallow.

"But this is the first book in this…uh…well, series, Pip. There *might* be a…uh… baby. Later. If there was…uh…a father."

"*Harry!*"

"I…uh…have to give up on a father, for now, Pip."

"*Harry! PLEASE!*"

"I think I've found a new…uh…apartment, too. I called about it and—"

It seemed as though everything simply froze in time at that moment. Even me. It seemed a long time before I found my voice and used it. "You don't mean in Erpzig, do you?"

"No, Pip. Not…uh…Erpzig."

"Harry!" I breathed, as the tears began. "Oh, Harry, you can't. You just can't!"

Harry sighed. "I can't stay, Pip. Not now. They're getting...uh...married, Pip."

I threw my arms around Harry and sobbed.

"It's okay, Pip. Jennifer will soon have him...uh...trained. You'll see. And Davey's really very...uh...nice."

"Did Mom tell you they were getting married?" Harry handed me a fist full of tissues and I blew my nose and wiped my eyes.

"No, but Davey told me he was buying her a...uh...ring."

"But, Harry, you can't move! What'll I do?"

"Pip, I *can't* stay! But I *can* be your...uh...sitter sometimes. You'll just have to remind me to...uh...come, that's all. And I don't want to miss any of your...uh...ball games."

I walked slowly out the door and down the steps and into the house.

"What's wrong with you?" asked Jennifer.

"Harry's getting another apartment," I said, and went upstairs. Jennifer followed me into my room. I climbed up onto my bed and stared at the ceiling.

"Why?" she asked, in a whisper. I didn't answer. I didn't need to. There was only one thing would make Harry move. "*But how does he know?*" she cried.

"David told him he was buying Mom a ring."

Jennifer said nothing. She just walked out of my room and a little while later I heard the back door close. And she didn't come in for lunch.

I went down and made some sandwiches. I took some over and set them on Harry's desk. Harry was still staring at the blank paper.

"Thanks, Pip," said Harry.

I gulped. Harry had noticed the sandwiches. That meant he couldn't work! Did he feel as badly as we did?

On the way down the steps I spotted Jennifer lying on the tree house floor. I went in the house, put the rest of the sandwiches in a bread bag and carried them up the ladder. I sat down next to her and handed her a sandwich.

"We'll get to keep the house," I said.

"Yah."

"Doesn't seem so important anymore," I said.

"No," Jennifer agreed.

We ate in silence.

"We're not supposed to be here, Jen," I reminded her. "Not until there's some walls or a railing or something."

"This is all there's ever going to be."

"*Jen!*"

"He's leaving. He's not going to finish the tree house."

"Yes, he will! You'll see!"

"No, he won't, Pip. He doesn't care anymore."

"*Yes, he does!*"

"No. This is OUR TIME OF NEED, Pip, and he's leaving."

"He said he'd be back. To sit for us and go to my ball games."

"Aw, Pip, people always say stuff like that."

"They do?"

"Look at Brenda and me. Best friends forever. We each wrote one letter! And we'd promised never to let a single week go by without writing. That was January. This is August."

"Harry's even more than a best friend, Jen."

"Our dad told me he'd be back. And he was our dad. Our real dad!"

I climbed down the ladder and went back to my room.

Jennifer stayed on the tree house floor for the rest of the day and all the next day. And the next day was Saturday.

"He'll ask her tonight," she declared. "And she'll say yes."

"How do you know?" I asked.

"Pip, girls just know these things. Accept it. Deal with it."

I didn't argue. I knew she was right. And I knew Mom would say yes.

Jennifer went back to the tree house.

Harry didn't come for supper.

"He said he'd come over after you and David left, Mom," I told her.

"Well, if he doesn't, you go over and get him, because if he's working he'll never remember." She set the table for two.

"Aren't you eating?" Jennifer asked, as she came in the door.

Mom shook her head. "I had a snack earlier. David and I are going out for a late supper."

"Where?" asked Jennifer.

"Antoines."

"That French place?" I asked.

"A special occasion?" Jennifer asked.

We both watched her face closely. Nothing.

"Yes, the French place, and no, nothing special."

Jennifer looked at me and shrugged.

"You like Antoines, Mom?" I asked.

"Oh, it's a lovely place, but…"

"Gee, what's not to like?" asked Jennifer.

"Oh, it's just that everything is so proper and perfect and you feel you have to be proper and perfect and you know you're not, and you feel if you just sneeze or something, it'll be some kind of criminal offence, or…" Mom shrugged. "I'm being silly, of course. It's a beautiful place and David is wonderful to take me. And it is a lovely treat. I just wouldn't want a steady diet, that's all."

Jennifer looked at me and raised her eyebrows.

"I was wondering," Mom said, "if you'd like to have David over for supper tomorrow. You don't know him very well, and perhaps we could have a barbeque. Something very relaxed and informal. I could make a huge bowl of potato salad."

"Sure, why not," said Jennifer, getting up from the table. "Can I go outside, now?"

"You've hardly eaten a thing!"

"Not hungry," Jennifer said.

"Me either," I said. In fact I felt downright sick. David for supper!

"What's wrong with you two, anyway? You've been moping around here all day."

"Harry's leaving," Jennifer said.

"What?" asked Mom, clearly not understanding. "What do you mean, leaving? On a holiday?"

"He's got another apartment, Mom," I said. Mom stared at us. She looked really peculiar. Was she just a shade green? "Can we go, now?"

"Yes, yes of course. It's time for me to get ready, too. And I still have to clear away the supper no one ate." She began to pick up dishes. She dropped a glass and water sprayed out over the floor. "Well, not broken, anyway."

We started out together, but I came back in. "You want some help, Mom?" I asked.

"No, Dear, that's fine. You run along and play," she said as she began to sponge up the water. I began to leave again. "Pip?"

"Yah, Mom?"

"You're sure about this?"

I nodded. I thought Mom looked like I felt. When I got outside, I found Jennifer standing under the tree house. The music of Beethoven drifted out of Harry's window. Harry was working.

"*We'll* finish it," Jennifer said, her voice quiet but firm.

"*The tree house?*"

"Right! Well, we're at least going to put up some rails. Come on."

So I handed boards up to Jennifer and Jennifer measured them and handed them back for me to saw.

"Aren't these boards for the walls, Jen?"

"Yah, but the other ones are too thick for you to saw. We'd be here forever if we used them."

"Oh." I figured there had to be a reason for Harry to have bought the other ones for the wall supports, but I wasn't going to argue. It was tough enough sawing these thin ones! Even so, I was almost able to keep up with Jennifer's hammering.

We finished the two ends. Jennifer bounced against them, "See? She cried. "They're really strong!" I nodded and grinned. "Now let's get this side done. It's the longest."

I began sawing a long thin board.

"Hurry up, Pip, it's almost time for David to get here."

"Maybe she'll say no, Jen. She doesn't *have* to say yes, does she?"

"Of course not! Jeepers Pip! But I know she'll say yes."

"Really?"

"Yah, really." And without me even asking her how she knew, she said, "Girls just know these things."

I cut through the long board and handed it up to Jennifer.

"Come on up, Pip. We'll watch for him from here. Then we can just wave. We won't have to go right over and talk or anything." I climbed the ladder and watched Jennifer hammer the second nail. "There! All done!"

"Don't you need to put more than one nail in each end, Jennifer?" I asked.

Jennifer gave me one of 'her looks'. "Don't be so wasteful." She looked at her watch. "We finished this railing just in time. Sixty…fifty-nine…fifty-eight…" counted Jennifer, and as she counted she bounced against the single long board that she'd just nailed in place.

"What are you doing?" I asked.

"I'm doing a countdown for David. When I reach zero, he'll be here." She looked back at her watch. "Twenty-one…twenty…nineteen…eighteen…"

And then it happened. I thought I heard a little squeak first, and then the crunch as the board broke and the nails pulled out all at the same time. And Jennifer fell! Her upper body hit a branch and then she fell, straight down, feet first. When her left leg hit the ground she screamed. And screamed. And screamed.

And I was screaming, "Jen! Jen!" as I scurried down the ladder.

And Harry was running down the garage steps screaming, "Jennifer! Jennifer!"

And Mom was running out of the house wearing her beautiful new dress and screaming, "Jennifer! My darling Jennifer!"

And over and above it all was the music of Beethoven.

Then Mom was cradling Jennifer in her arms and Harry was asking Jennifer where it hurt. Then Harry said, "I think her leg's... uh...broken, Susan. Badly."

And then David was towering above us. "What's going on? Are you *late again?*"

"Jennifer's broken her leg!" cried Mom.

"Oh, I'm sorry," said David, but I didn't think he really was. And Jennifer was still screaming.

"David," Mom said, "we've got to take her to the hospital at once."

"Yes, of course," he said, but I thought he looked angry.

"*NO!*" screamed Jennifer, clutching Harry. "I want Harry!"

"Well, there you are," said David, smiling. "She wants Harry. You don't mind, do you, old man?"

"*What are you saying?*" cried Mom.

Jennifer stopped screaming and began whimpering. I thought she sounded a lot like Spike did when Fluffy attacked him. "Hey!" I cried. "Ever since Fluffy got Spike, Spike's left us alone." But everyone ignored me.

"David," Mom said. "We are taking Jennifer to the hospital in your car."

"She's not bleeding, is she?" asked David, with a glance towards his car.

"I want *HARRY*!" screamed Jennifer, trying to sit up and falling back down again.

"I'm only doing as your daughter asks," David said.

"*David*!"

"Look, Susan, it's not as though she's bleeding to death. She broke a leg. End of story. Harry can take her. That's what she wants."

"I think she wants her…uh…mother, too," put in Harry. Jennifer nodded, whimpering.

"David, just what are you *saying*?" Mom asked again, as Harry carefully lifted Jennifer and carried her toward David's big Chrysler.

"I'm saying I have *plans*, Susan, *big plans*."

"And I don't give a fig Newton about your *plans*, right now, David," Mom said, trotting after Harry and Jennifer. I ran ahead and opened the back door of the Chrysler for Harry.

"But, Susan, they're very *special* plans!" cried David, trotting after Mom.

Mom crawled into the back seat and sat on the floor cradling Jennifer.

"The keys…uh…old man," said Harry.

"What keys?" asked David.

"Here are my…uh…car keys," said Harry as he placed his keys in David's hand. "Now give me yours."

"*What?*"

Harry put his hand on David's shoulder and I could see Harry's knuckles turn white as he pressed his fingers into David's flesh. David looked at Harry's hand and then at Harry. Harry's face looked a lot like a stone carving. "She needs your big back seat, David. Now give me your keys." He spoke slowly and carefully without the usual pauses.

Grudgingly David gave Harry his keys and I hopped in the front seat of the big Chrysler.

"Susan, this was going to be a *very special night!*" David cried as Harry turned the key in the ignition.

"Well, I'm sorry to disappoint you, David," called Mom as Harry put the car into gear. "But I seem to be a little busy just now."

"*I bought you a ring, Susan!*" David screamed as Harry slowly backed the Chrysler up.

"*Stick your ring!*" screamed Mom as Harry turned the car and pulled away. I turned and smiled at Jennifer. Through her tears, she smiled back.

"*Harry!*" yelled David. "Where are you taking *my car?*"

Harry stopped at the stop sign and then slowly inched forward as David ran onto the road, waving his arms and screaming.

Harry took all the corners slowly. He gently stopped for all the red lights.

"Why are you going so slowly?" I asked.

"Don't…uh…want to make Jennifer's pain worse by…uh…jarring her," Harry said.

I smiled at Harry and settled back in my seat.

Chapter Sixteen

WHEN JENNIFER WOKE UP

Harry and I waited for Mom.

"It's a compound fracture," she said when she saw us. "They're going to put her to sleep."

We waited some more. Mom. Harry. Me.

"She's going to be all right, Harry," Mom said.

"I know, but it's all my…uh…fault. All her pain! It didn't…uh…need to happen."

"It isn't your fault!" Mom repeated for the zillionth time. Of course it wasn't, I thought. It was Jennifer's.

Harry sighed and sat down next to Mom. "I just wanted them to have…uh…a tree house. Like I did."

"I know," said Mom and she took Harry's hand in hers.

"I just…uh…wanted them to have a place away from us adults, that's all. A place that was…uh…theirs to share. A place to go and think and…uh…dream."

"And you gave them that, Harry. And it's not your fault. It's Jennifer's fault."

Yes! Jennifer's!

"Oh, no, I—"

"No, Harry, it *was* Jennifer's fault. She shouldn't have been doing what she was doing. She didn't have the least notion what she was doing, but she went ahead and did it anyway. That's Jennifer. She's always going ahead on her own. She never asks."

I wondered what Mom would say if she only knew what else Jennifer had been doing without asking!

"She's so headstrong," Mom continued. "She never bothers to find out the facts. She just takes off and does whatever. Sometimes it all works out. Sometimes it doesn't. And, unfortunately, Harry, sometimes when things don't work out, it hurts. It hurts a lot."

Harry nodded and then they were silent. They were silent for a long time. But Mom and Harry held hands the whole time they waited. The doctor came at last and said Jennifer was fine but was still asleep. We all went and looked at her sleeping. She was snoring but only faintly.

"You might as well go home and get some rest," the nurse advised us.

"I'd rather wait," Mom replied, patting Jennifer's arm. "Why don't you two go down to the cafeteria?"

"Yah! I'm starving." My appetite had returned about the time we'd left David.

We started to leave, and suddenly Mom was flinging her arms around Harry's neck. "Oh, Harry!" she cried, looking up at him. "I just realized something!"

"What?"

"When all this happened you were working, weren't you? I heard your music, so you must have been!"

"Yes," said Harry. "I...uh...guess I was, but—"

"Don't you see?" asked Mom.

Suddenly Harry's face broke into a huge grin. He hugged Mom tightly and I could tell Mom was really hugging Harry hard! "I heard the baby cry!" he whispered.

Mom wiped her eyes. "You did, *you really did*!"

"Harry?" I asked when we sat down in the cafeteria. "You can put yourself in the painting now, can't you?"

Harry grinned. "Maybe I…uh…can."

Jennifer was still mostly asleep when we got back to the room, so Harry and I went for a walk around the parking lot. We soon discovered that the Chrysler was gone and Harry's bent up sports car was parked in it's place.

"Been thinking I should see about getting…uh…a bigger car," Harry said as we walked up to it. There was an envelope taped to the windshield.

"What's it say" I asked when Harry peeled it off.

"'You probably need this more than me', it says." Harry opened the envelope. There was a diamond ring inside.

"I looked longingly up at Harry. "Do you?" I asked, my voice squeaking just a little.

"Nope!" said Harry, and he tossed the ring away.

My stomach lurched. My legs felt very much like jelly.

"*I'll pick out the ring myself, thank you very much, David*!" he yelled to the night sky.

I jumped up and down, screeching, "Really? *REALLY*?"

"Well, if it's…uh…okay with you and Jennifer."

"It is, Harry! It really is!"

He picked me up and swung me around. "Of course, your… uh…Mom might have something to…uh…say about it."

"Yah, I guess."

"I should probably…uh…take her out to…uh…Antoines a few times and stuff like that."

"Yah, but not Antoines, Harry."

"No?"

"No."

"But other places?"

"Yah."

"We'll find our...uh...own places."

I nodded and Harry got down on the ground and began crawling around on all fours. "Whatcha doing, Harry?"

"Well, maybe I do...uh...need that ring, Pip."

"You don't need it, Harry."

Harry got up. "Sure?"

I grinned. "Positive!"

When we got back to Jennifer's room she was awake.

"Thanks, Harry," Jennifer said, in a very small voice. Then she smiled at him.

Harry just smiled and kissed her on the forehead, and in a little while, we began to say our good nights.

"Mom, can Pip stay just another minute?" Jennifer asked.

"Certainly, Dear." And Mom and Harry were gone.

"At least we got rid of David," Jennifer said. "We did, didn't we?" I nodded. "I was thinking, Pip, that tomorrow I'll start asking the nurses about which doctor is married and which one isn't and if they're—"

"Jen?"

"Yah?"

"Never mind."

"Too late, huh?" Jennifer sighed. "I guess I kinda knew it all along. I mean, you gotta love the nut." I grinned. "I don't know, though. Does he make enough to pay the rent *and* the increased cost of the mortgage *and* his other expenses?"

"Jen, if they're married he won't be renting the apartment."

"Oh, yes he will!" cried Jennifer, pulling herself up and then flopping back down again.

"Of course he won't!" I cried. "He and Fluffy will live in the house with us."

"Yah, right," agreed Jennifer, "but he's *not working* in the house! His *work* stays in the apartment. I'm not having that mess in our house!"

"Right."

"I just hope he can afford it, that's all."

Should I tell her? Nah. Maybe later. Nah. I didn't think I should. If Jennifer knew she'd just keep scheming to get more and more stuff out of Harry. More and more Barbie stuff! And soon our house would be just like Harry's apartment. But instead of wading through scrumpled up papers and old painty clothes, we'd be wading through Barbie junk. Endless Barbie junk!

Nope. I'm not going to tell her, I decided. Not ever.

And I haven't.

www.ingramcontent.com/pod-product-compliance
Lightning Source LLC
LaVergne TN
LVHW041813060526
838201LV00046B/1251